BLACK LIGHT

BLACK LIGHT

Laura Solomon

First published in New Zealand in 1996 by
TANDEM PRESS
2 Rugby Road, Birkenhead, North Shore City,
New Zealand.

ISBN 0 908884 80 X

Designed by Suellen Allen
Typeset by Egan Reid Ltd, Auckland
Printed in New Zealand by Wright and Carman (NZ) Ltd, Upper Hutt

The publishers gratefully acknowledge the assistance of Creative New Zealand

CONTENTS

Acknowledgements

The author wishes to thank: Lenore Brady, the Brodie family, Mel Johnston, Sue McCauley, Margaret Mahy, Rochelle Savage, the Solomon family, Lucy Somerville and Kate Tarrant.

Thanks also to Jane Parkin for her editorial assistance.

The author wishes to acknowledge the following as inspiration:

Faulkner, William *The Sound and the Fury* (Chatto and Windus Ltd, Great Britain, 1931)

Gardam, Jane *Queen of the Tambourine* (Sinclair-Stevenson Ltd, London, 1991)

The quotation '*Light of my life, fire of my lions*' is from Nabokov, Vladimir *Lolita* (Weidenfeld and Nicolson Ltd, Great Britain, 1959)

The quotation 'Every step you take, every move you make' is from *Every Breath You Take*, The Police Greatest Hits (A&M Records Ltd, London)

ACKNOWLEDGEMENTS

I

Willy

Everything was silent. Everything was blue. The ice in the water was cold. *Down the brown path and through the gap in the hedge the ragged rascal ran.* Something green was on fire. The dog was on fire. *The lamp flashed white.* The sky was orange and fading away. The dog was howling. The dog was burning in the street. *The glass was breaking against the wall.* The sun was black. *The sun was white.* The man went through the ceiling, out past the holes of light. *The big brown dog jumped over the white haired girl.* The lamp was silent. The lamp was black.

'Don't get me wrong. I loved my father. I always had. I wouldn't have had a word said against him. But, oh, he was a mean stinking son of a bitch. He could be crueller than any bloke I know. My uncle reckoned it was 'cause he didn't have the nice feminine influence around to cool him down and make him sweet and kind and giving. My uncle seemed to think that if Pop had only had a small bit to bake him hot apple pies and scrub the grime from his shirt collars, it would've all been all right.

Of course, said my uncle, my father had always fancied the fallen whores and their flashing red lamps, and had never been interested in the saintly types. As a child, I was spoon-fed the propaganda that his mean nature was the consequence of a misspent youth, a youth revolving around the brothels and bars of Plymouth. I believed this for a short time. When I got older, like, I decided that he'd just been born mean and that he'd stay that way till the day he died.

Of course the boys and I had done stuff before. Different stuff. Pop often said that I was a follower, which was and wasn't true. Kylo was the leader, we'd all agreed to that at some stage or another, voluntarily or not. But I knew how to make, like, decisions on my own and stuff. When we were out working, if I thought things were going to start looking messy then I'd usually hang back and let someone else do the job. Not that I was afraid or nothing. Just I didn't agree with violence for the sake of it, but only as a way of serving our overall purpose. Mind you, if one of the boys looked as though they was getting in a spot of bother, I'd be right in there, black boots flying and kicking, no need to tell me twice.

It was just old folks mostly, ones that looked like they'd never had to lick the grease off no one's shoes. Nor rub up no one's floor till it gleamed like the bathroom mirror, nor chop firewood by torchlight till 3.35 am, then be back at school the next day after that. They was the ones we targeted, really. The ones with a bit of dosh. We never did them over too harshly neither, unless one of us was in a real nasty, nasty mood. Then we'd really put the boot in. Then we put the boot in till it gleamed, and we'd run away to leave the old bugger screaming and moaning for help, our boots leaving bloody tracks behind them. 'Less it was a store and they was putting up resistance or trying to ring the old bluebells or something. Then we'd get out the old black instrument, and pretend like we was just a bit trigger happy. But we never used it. We just waved it around in the air like a magician's wand, till we got what we wanted. Then we'd split.

But I never put a spade through no one's head. Till tonight. When you do somebody like that, it goes red, then it goes black, then it goes white. If you look out the window you can see the white lines. Flashing past, like somebody's trying to race us to elsewhere. Only they're headed in the wrong direction.'

I swung back on my chair and surveyed the group of friends, relishing the small space of silence.

'Well?'

Buckell imitated my posture. 'I wouldn't buy it.'

Buckell is one of my closest friends, and I admire his fine New Physics mind, but sometimes he can be an awful arsehole.

'I'm not asking you to buy it, Buckell. I'm asking you to evaluate it as a piece of literature. I want you to assess it in purely objective terms.'

Timmo chimed in. 'Surely you want it to sell. What's the point of writing the darned thing if it doesn't sell a couple of copies?'

Two medium-sized bits of fibreboard have more intelligence than Timmo. He thinks in terms of lager, mince pies and sex.

'If I was aiming for the bestseller lists, I'd write a doctor and nurse romance. I want you to think about the aesthetics of the piece.'

'I quite enjoyed parts of it,' said Larkin. 'The bit about the lines running the wrong way. Near the end. I had a giggle about that.'

Buckell drained the last of his lager. 'Keep at it, old thing. Everybody needs their little outlet. Like to see you finish it, though I think we both know how likely that is. But that doesn't matter. Sounds like the kind of work that would date terribly anyhow. And isn't it largely derivative? It sounds very familiar. Why don't you try and do something kind of futuristic and sci-fi. Sort of a Phillip K. Dick.'

'I've got another manuscript coming along actually, now that you mention it. I don't believe in working on just one piece. I find it limits one's sense of . . . '

'Got another page or two up your sleeve then, have you? Come on then, delight us, baby-boy.' Buckell was using a match to remove a piece of meat from between his molars.

'It's my attempt at the opposite gender,' I said, feeling slightly sick at the prospect of laying my artist's soul bare in the Big Girl's Arms at 5.15 on a Monday night as businessmen hurried home outside the window.

Timmo whistled long and low.

'It's set at a circus.'

'Top marks for originality, old thing, top marks.'

'Half of it. The other half is sort of suburban malaise.'

'Opposite gender. He means girls.'

'Women,' I interjected. 'I mean women.'

'I like the sound of that,' said Larkin. 'That has a nice ring to it. *Women Of The Circus Ring*. Wearing G-strings and lace. Make a good porno.'

'Is this your second story, or the one you just read us?' asked Buckell, ''cause that didn't sound like a circus housewife to me. That was more like *One Goes Mad In Plymouth*.'

'It's a separate story. I said that.'

'Women and elephants, yeah, I like the thought of that. Especially small Thai girls. I can see that. *Fifi At The Carnival*. That'd really sell.'

'Let him get on with it.'

I cleared my throat, and shot the barlady a look that suggested she should bring me another lager, pronto. She was a good girl really, and never gave us much trouble, even slipped us the occasional free pint when the mood took her. I gave the boys my most searing look, and put on my poshest accent.

'It's a piss-take,' I said, 'sort of.'

'Dear Carry,
I really do think you should come back home. The Street misses you dreadfully, and I have heard Mrs Grange say that we all might agree to forget about the whole incident if you would just return home before the thirty-first of this month. I'm not one to

pick out faults in others, Carry, but you *have* been terribly selfish. God knows, I used to be similar myself. Selfishness is a terrible, sinful thing. It is the worm inside the apple and the blight inside the pear. You must eradicate this evil from your life, and return to your neighbourhood to resume your wifely duties. Your house and garden are suffering from neglect. How the begonias droop and the geraniums wilter in the scorching summer sun! To say nothing of the red tulips, who bleed into the cracks created in the parched soil. Neglect, Carry, is also a sin, being a kindred cousin of Sloth. Remember! If one gets into the habit of forgetting to cleanse one's oven one week, then one might never be able to successfully cleanse an oven again. A germ could find a loving home and breed with a sense of purpose. My old mother (God bless her immaculate soul) always used to say that cleanliness was next to godliness, and it only takes one small peek into your refrigerator to see that you have become a fallen child of the rotting sourcream-and-onion dip variety.

And another thing. Your own personal zoo. Well, I have taken a firm stance on this, and under no circumstances whatsoever shall I agree to take over as keeper. I have not seen the spaniel for days, and refuse to conduct a search for him, although I have alerted the local members of Neighbourhood Watch. And if he comes home I shall not feed him. I say this not to be cruel, Caroline, but rather to be kind, to induce you to return to the Street, if not for the sake of your family, then for the sake of your pets. The chickens peck and strut their way around the dusty yard, cooped up and oozing frustration out of every feather. I give them no feed; they forage for what they can. However, despite this stance, I have deigned to make an exception of the goldfish, for of all the animals they seem to be feeling your absence the most violently. An aura of melancholy exudes from the fishbowl like a haze of navy blue cloud.

Your disappearance is irresponsible beyond words. If we have said or done anything to offend you, you should have made your hurt clear at the time. You are carrying on like a fourteen-year-old. I hear you ride elephants. I hope your body is decently covered, Carry, when you perform.

I must go and wipe away the froth from the dirty oven now, but I shall write again soon, to plead the case on behalf of the Street.

Until then, I shall remain faithfully yours,

Patricia Gluckendown'

'Been reading Jane Gardam, have you?' asked Buckell.

'Shut up,' said Larkin. 'Let the boy speak.'

Buckell wouldn't know originality if it jumped up and clouted him in the gob. Disdainfully, I washed out my mouth with fresh lager. 'New page,' I said. 'Every letter begins on a fresh page.'

'That's good,' said Larkin. 'A feeling of actual letters. Then the readers get real intimate with the narrator, and can jerk off with twice the cataclysmic power.'

'I can't see the academics going for it, myself. They don't go in for that sort of anguished repressed housewife stuff. And neither do I.'

'Shut up, Buckell. He's not going for academia, he's hoping for sex-shop.'

'You promised it was about girls,' said Timmo.

'It *is*.'

Larkin made a bid for silence, as Buckell casually flicked through a copy of *Black Holes and Baby Universes*.

'I'm not reading another instalment until I have your complete attention.'

'Sorry. It really is first rate. Better than that *Mad In*

Plymouth bit we began with. Keep up with the fish symbolism.'

'It's not a symbol.'

'Right. Metaphor, literary allusion, whatever.' He glanced at his watch. 'Gotta be off in five minutes, so let's hear another bit, eh Jimbob?'

'Dear Carry,
How are the elephants? I hear you wear a skimpy outfit coated in pink sequins. You will be careful, won't you, with those huge big trunks and all. I remember how you used to struggle with your vacuum cleaner. Mrs Grange came around to visit today, and we talked for a full hour about the implications of your escapade. We concluded that we are still in shock, and have not yet come to terms with the consequences of your actions. Gary is in a terrible mess about the whole thing. Mrs Grange saw him yesterday, and said that his shirt was untucked and his black umbrella had a tear in it, where the rain was pouring through. Of course he puts on a brave front for all of us, but he is slipping on the little things, the everyday repairs and ordering, the getting out of bed in the morning with a smile, the mending of rips and tears. The cleansing of an oven. As I said, the responsibility for the goldfish has been loaded on to me. I have been very good about everything, says Mrs Grange, what with having Gary around to tea every second night, and picking up the children from ballet and gymnastics and Scouts and Brownies. And feeding the fish. They don't look healthy, Carry. The one with tiger-stripes, in particular, no longer swims in quite the same little circles it used to. It is all I can manage to keep him healthy and interested in life. (The goldfish, not Gary, although perhaps that too.)

As you frisk happily with the striped tigers, think

of what you have left behind, and the trail of havoc you have created in your wake. I hope my letters may convince you that your rightful place is back here among friends and neighbours who love and respect you. How much respect can you possibly get from those sideshow freaks?

And let us not forget, my dearest Caroline, that *respect* for one's neighbour is as a foundation of concrete for a shack of straw. Without the basics (respect, moral standards, decent hygiene, etc, etc, etc), we are as the frail skeletons of leaves, buffeted on the breezes issuing forth from beneath the wings of the West Wind's cape. You are as a tiny elm leaf at present, at the mercy of every gust. You are waiting for the wolf to puff down your small shack and eat you up. I *know* this for a fact. Oh, yes I do. I have my *eye* on you, Carry. Every step you take and every move you make, I am *watching*. I spy, I have an EYE, I have an EYE on you.

This is how I *know*. This is how I know exactly how you live your life, out there amongst all that our neighbourhood has ordered itself against. I hired *him*. To report back to me, and to inform me as to your nefarious activities. This 'check' is for your own good. For what if you were to leave the country completely, Carry? And don't try and tell me that it hasn't happened. I know what becomes of these circus types once they get an idea into their heads. They become rash and impetuous, destroying the neat order of their own lives and crashing heedlessly through the patterned lives of others. The freaks have led you astray, my dear, and I have taken it upon myself to see that you are brought safely back to the nest. I speak to you through the Voice of Experience. I hope that you feel secure in the knowledge that the Street knows what you are up to.

I shall post this now, so as it reaches you by

Monday. I keep track of the circus. I have marked its movements upon my wall calendar.

Your concerned friend,
Patricia Gluckendown'

'Dearest Caroline,
I have just received the second report of your behaviour and whereabouts. I'm shocked. Shocked and disgusted. I have included a photocopy of the letter, so that you may see how frivolous your new life appears to those who are outside looking in. I have not had the heart to show this letter to Gary, as I fear the shock would trigger off his bowel problems. Even Mrs Grange I do not consider fully equipped to contemplate the contents of this letter and still remain mentally sound.

Gary came over for dinner last night and nearly saw the letter lying open on the kitchen table. Luckily I put the eel pie down on top of it, before he had time to pick it up and examine it. He appears to be awfully thin. I doubt that he eats properly. He devoured three helpings of the pie and mash, and seemed so keen on the thing that I packaged the rest of it up in gladwrap and sent him on his way. He must have looked quite a sight, running across the Street with half a fish pie stuffed down his shirt in order to keep it out of the rain. He is not himself.

How can I put this? He needs a woman. I can only provide him with so much. We don't mention your name, but stick politely to neutral topics such as his binding business and my little part-time job at the hospital. You could benefit from a job such as mine, Carry. When my boys grew up and left home, I found myself with a lot of spare time on my hands. Meals On Wheels helped me to cope with this difficult transitional period. Selflessness is a wonderful thing. You could take a leaf or two out of my book and think about devoting your life to others, as I have done, or been forced to do. Still, that is enough about me.

I hope you may appreciate the hurt and dismay I felt upon receiving this report of your circumstances and whereabouts. The circus moves not as I had mapped it on my calendar. I shall have to be very careful not to lose track of you.

I found the circus caravans parked on a small common just outside Wainui. They had positioned themselves near a middling sized river, and several of the workers were stripped off and bathing themselves. I identified the case in question by her red hair. She appears to have changed her name to Caro. She was laughing and joking quite openly with her workmates. She was in fine physical condition, and has suffered neither physically nor mentally from working with such a crew. They bathed for approximately ten minutes, during which time I averted my eyes as I thought appropriate. Dinner was prepared and served at 18:25. The night's show was scheduled to start at 20:00.

The crowd attracted was not a particularly large one, and seemed to be largely composed of young people and businessmen. The act of the case in question was preceded by a cheap trick involving a 'magician' calling himself Godiver, a chainsaw and a buxom blonde girl in a box. The girl appeared relatively unharmed by the trick, although she was subjected to numerous lecherous glares from the direction of the 'magician'.

The case is not a rider of elephants as was first supposed. The elephants are ridden by a woman who has been part of the circus for over forty years, and is a mute. Her costume consists of pink sequins and barely covers her essential regions.

The act of the case was third on the programme, following on from:

(a) The 'magician' Godiver and his blonde accomplice.

(b) The rider of elephants.

The case performs her show without nets, in a costume consisting only of flesh-coloured lycra. Several trapezes are involved, as is a tightrope. Dry ice is expelled upwards, towards the case, from the floor of the main circus tent, creating an atmosphere of smog, and causing several members of the audience, including myself, to cough profusely.

The case shows no fear, nor does she at any stage during the performance cast her eyes downwards. Her gaze appears to be fixated on a point in space approximately one metre in front of her eyes. She wears no jewellery. The show did not appear to be a particularly popular part of the circus, with most of the audience wandering off to refresh themselves with sticky pink candy floss, orange drink and bleeding sausages on sticks. The show lasted exactly 29 minutes, from 21:07 until 21:36.

The case appears to be performing six shows at Wainui, after which time the circus will slowly be heading north to perform in seven other centres before leaving the country to tour Australia. It is advised to try and contact the case at the address below, before the year ends and the circus heads overseas.

Report ended.

You can see, Carry, why I took such pains to conceal the letter from the downcast eyes of your husband, Gary. Also Mrs Grange, with her boys on the rugby field and her hair in rollers. I hate to say this, but you have reduced yourself to a kind of hooker. I cannot write much more for today. The thought of you walking and swinging across a smoggy abyss for forty-eight nights does nothing for my nerves. I shall have to take two dispirin, and lie down upon the sofa with a cup of Earl Grey.

Patricia Gluckendown'

Timmo stood up and began to urinate into a nearby pot plant, unseen by the barlady.

'It's not exactly *Do Androids Dream of Electric Sheep?*, is it?' said Buckell, readjusting his own belt so as to accommodate the pint he had consumed.

Larkin tenderly wiped a tear from his eye. The

effects of the alcohol were starting to show.

Timmo's buttocks smacked back down against his vinyl seat. 'Where does this Patricia live then?' He waved to the barlady to bring him one steak and cheese pie with sauce and one chicken and apricot pie with no sauce.

'Which one you like better, Timmo?'

'Steak and cheese, any day.'

I decided it was best to ignore him.

'Larkin?'

Larkin snivelled softly. 'The one about Fifi. It's very moving.'

'Buckell?'

'I don't think you're hitting the nail on the head with either of them. If you want my honest opinion, I don't know why you bother.' He tugged at the waistline of his trousers. 'Well, I've done my dash. See you blokes same time tomorrow.' He drained the dregs of his beer.

'You boys are pathetic. You wait till I send this away.'

'We'll wait,' said Buckell, smiling a slow and slimy smile to himself, 'we'll wait a long, long time. We'll wait for ever.'

I upended my own beer and left the Big Girl's Arms feeling slightly despondent and down at heel.

My mother greeted me at the front door, and clipped my ear.

'You stink of booze. Your tea's gone cold in the pot. You're lucky we didn't feed it to the dog. You lazy shit. When was the last time you went out looking for a job? We ain't gonna support you till you're dead. Sooner or later you is going to have to get off your arse and find yourself a proper job with proper wages that can feed a man and clothe a man. Sooner or later *you'* (she delivered me another fine belt to the left ear as she uttered the second person pronoun) 'is going to have to stop nicking our kitty from out of the jam jar and going out boozing.'

The tops of my shoes were slightly scuffed. The left one had a small patch where the surface of the leather had been scratched away to reveal the light brown hide which lurked beneath. The right one gleamed slightly from where some of Timmo's urine had splattered. I rubbed one shoe against the other in a nervous manner.

'And you can get a rag from the garage and give those boots a decent bloody polishing.'

I moved in through the front door into the lounge. My brother sat crouched on the carpet, spoon-feeding himself. Stewed apple was bubbling out of his mouth and flowing like lava on to the front of his shirt, mingling happily with the Marmite stains which lay coagulating from that morning's meal. Red was watching the cricket with a beer balanced delicately on his gut. He grunted. I bumped the sofa with my knee and beer sloshed out on to his crotch. He grunted again.

I climbed the staircase to my room in the attic. The staircase is narrow and the steps are small. The banister is imitation polished oak, the ends furling under like fern fronds. According to the previous owners, both staircase and banister narrowly escaped the Great Fire of '54. Upstairs had been reduced to a hollow charcoal shell, gutted. A blackened cicada casing. The story went that some lodger with pyromaniac intentions had set fire to his room, then thrown himself, nightgown ablazing, from his window, landing in a soft drift of snow, thereby narrowly escaping his intended death. My room has a history.

The moment I stepped inside my door, I knew that Mum had been in cleaning things. I could tell, 'cause my records had been picked up from across the floor and neatly stacked in one corner, next to the stereo. I threw on some Bach and turned up the volume. Then I turned the volume up again. The glass of the window panes began to rattle. I could hear Mum screaming from down in the kitchen. Willy was howling into his apple. Then I turned the volume up a third time and I couldn't hear anything beyond the door any more, and all I could hear was Bach rising and falling, rising and falling in waves of light. Mass in B Minor. Took him five years to write that. Silly bastard.

Then her face flashed before me as a beam of light. Soft blonde hair framing a heart-shaped face. Delicate pink hands passing melting ice creams across the counter. The soft glow of the ice-cream reflecting off her forehead. And yet not a pimple on her. *Light of my life, fire of my loins.* My little Lepidoptera.

Then I passed out.

I came to with Mum yelling at me from out in the back lawn where she was hanging out her white sheets. I pulled down my window, locked my door and got out my first manuscript. Bloody Buckell and his *One Goes Mad In Plymouth*. Watches too many TV re-runs, does our Buckell. This was no kid's-book parody, this was English Psycho, very close to the United States version. I must confess, I've never actually read *American Psycho*, but the title definitely has a good ring about it, as Larkin would say. It's catchy. Josephine Public likes to read about the mentally disturbed. It gives her a warm satisfied glow. This was what I was trying to deliver to the reader of my work. A feeling of satisfaction, like they'd just been at the pub with some mates for a few hours and had a couple of pints and a pork pie, and were looking forward to a night out, with perhaps a bit of beaver at the end of it. They could read about all these people who had done evil things,

things which had transgressed social order, and they could then feel all right about themselves. They could go home at the end of the night, and feel as if they were somehow cleaner and cleverer than the next man. That's what I wanted for my reader, anyway. You can see what a selfless guy I am.

'Kylo had his hands on the wheel and was careering around like a mad thing. Even my girl could have driven better than that. All I could keep my mind on now was the body we had packed up in the trunk. It would be well stiff by now. Stiff as a rod of iron. Kylo's steering was making the white lines slither like crazy snakes across the tarseal. All I could think to myself was, 'Well, you're in the shit now, boyo.' I didn't speak out loud, in case I made Kylo angry and he told me to shut the fuck up, like he had three times already.

I tried to think of the corpse as a thing far removed from my father, as a concrete doll quartered into not-so-neat portions. I hoped Pop had made it to heaven. He'd preached enough about hell in his time. Hopefully this had exorcised the infernal regions from his soul. White lines kept passing. Bugs flew in through the open window and popped on the interior light, sizzling as they fell. In my lap lay a small black morgue.

'Roll up that window, willya?'

I obeyed. To tell the honest-to-God truth, I had been kinda scared of Kylo. Shit scared, actually. The killing was all his fucking fault. If he hadn't been there yelling in my ear, like he shoulda been perched on my shoulder with horns on his head, I would have dealt old Pop a couple of blows with the jackhammer, and that would have been that. Concussion and perhaps a spot of damage to the thinking box, then a right hiding for me when Pop came round. But oh no, we hadn't just stopped at concussion. He'd pushed me on, old Kylo had, yelling, 'Get the spade into 'im, get the spade into 'im!' Yelling, 'Go on – slice his head open like a pumpkin! Remember when he made you chop wood all through the night?' By then I was seeing red, and it was too late to stop. I had to take the life out of the old bugger, like he had taken the life out of me. Kylo had pushed me to the old edge, Kylo had. To stop myself from falling, I had to kill Pop. The other kids had been standing back by that point. Just watching. Watching me and watching Kylo watching me. I didn't want to keep going then, but I had gone too far, had been really laying into the old bugger, and Kylo was liking it pretty good, yelling along in time with the thumps of the spade, with the spit flying out of the corners of his mouth.

From where I was sitting in the back seat, I could see the clock on the dashboard ticking over very, very slowly. The rearview mirror suspended from the roof had a slight crack in it, so that Kylo's face appeared as if split in half by a stray hair. Kylo's hair is very dark, and falls in waves across his shoulders. He loves it to death, that son of a bitch. I once saw Monty spit from a second storey window on to Kylo's hair. The next day Monty had a black eye and a limp.

Before the murder, I had been scared of Kylo. Now I was still scared, only I couldn't help wondering what Kylo would look like bald, and old, with sags of skin buckling helplessly over his trousers. When somebody is standing so close to the fire that they think they're red hot, it's damn tempting to get a poker and ram it up their arse and shove them right in there among the coal. That's what I was thinking now, anyway. 'Cause before I'd been scared of Kylo, but right now I was just terrified of the law, and of the ghost of Pop. Pop had never been a great one for long-distance travel. Especially not in pieces, in a suitcase, in the boot of a rusted brown Holden with one door nearly falling off. And I had never been handy with a spade. But tonight I was gonna have to be even handier than last night, 'cause I knew that Kylo wasn't gonna be caught dead digging no burial hole.'

I liked it. I thought the slang and swearwords were kind of a nifty touch, adding panache, flamboyance and realism. Also a nice feminist touch with the reference to 'my girl' fairly early on in the piece, showing not only that such an ignoramus could have the same girl for more than one night but also that he respected her driving. Or, alternatively, highlighting the way in which such oafs treated their women. I wondered if it would be a bestseller; perhaps a candidate for the Booker Prize, or else sold on all the right stands in international airports. I toyed with the idea of introducing sex scenes, perhaps a sensitive portrayal of female sexuality. Or at least a few descriptions of naked women. However, I had never seen a real live naked living doll, so felt that the dark continent was an area of expertise best left untouched in fiction until explored in real life.

What would *she* think of it? Could I take it to her, show her, press it into her hands? No, no, never. Though in all truth I wrote to please her, my angel, to satisfy her and quench her thirst with words of . . . love? No, not love, but only to please her. Yet, she'd never read it. No, not to be read by those deep violet eyes, sheltering behind their luscious dark lashes. Never to snatch my papers back in shame, and run out on to the beach, away, far away from her and her scent. Honeysuckle, mmm, honeysuckle, sweet and dripping into the hokey pokey ice-cream, her voluptuous body pressing against the counter, the rustle of her skirts against her silken thighs, her bending over to pick up a stray object from the floor . . . oh, my little nymphet. I rubbed myself frantically against the bedpost.

Bash, bash, bash.

Red was beating his stomach against my door in order to attract my attention.

'What's going on in there, son?'

He rattled the door handle, then belched loudly.

'Studying, Father.'

'Don't you "Father" me! I know exactly what you're doing in there with that blasted music! Open up this instant, or you'll have your mother up and climbing in through the window.'

The thought of my mother climbing in through my bedroom window truly terrified me, and so I opened my door to stand face to face with my obesely overfleshed 'father'.

'Git yourself down to the breakfast table, boy, and git some decent grub into ya for a change. By crikey I know how you lads all fill y'selves up with brandy and beer and can't even squeeze down a good morning's porridge. Don't think your mother and I don't know what you get up to when you're not at home with us. Jeez, boy, your mother has her hands full with that brother of yours, and you can't even get out there in the workforce to help support the family. You'd think that with a brother like that, and what with your father doing himself . . . ' He broke off. Red knows about brow-beating from the sacrosanct. 'The Lord has sent this family a double burden to bear. We can't do much about your father, he having opted out of this world and moved into the next, but we can all help out with Willy. I won't say he isn't a trial. But we've coped with him, as a family we've coped with him. And we pay Diana to take care of him as many hours as we can afford. Now, son, we expect you to do your share, to use the skills and the wit your brother never received.'

I composed my face into a placating facade. 'I shall shower and be down shortly.'

This seemed to satisfy him, for he belched again in a companionable sort of a way and waddled off down the staircase. I felt the floorboards shudder with each thud of his tremendous feet.

They weren't bad really, Mum and Red, considering their limited education. And it wasn't easy, having Willy in the family. That was part of the problem really. I think they were all jealous of the fact that I had gone to a school of higher learning. Dad reckoned BA stood for Bugger All, but I assured him it was the only degree of any real importance for a man in today's world. An English education, I said, equips one for *life.* Without it, one is hollow and incomplete; one's fellow man is a mystery to one. The well-read man is in a position to sympathise with his planetary co-inhabitants, as well as explain to any eager listener at a pub or party the consequences and implications of French feminist theory, semiotics, postmodernism and abjection.

Red's a taxi driver. I told him his life was in a rut. He told me I was an arrogant little twat. I love my folks. They only charge me thirty dollars board.

When I arrived in the kitchen Mum was putting a loaf together. She has a problem with the pre-packaged supermarket loaf, my mother does. She makes part wholemeal, part white, so that Willy gets his healthy stuff and Red doesn't complain that he's eating brick-loaf. Mum says she doesn't want her kids poisoned with additives. So I eat the maximum amount of red food colouring when I'm away from her. Only once Willy got hold of a packet of Sparkles I had in my bedroom and it triggered him off and I got into the shit.

Mum splattered some grey porridge into a bowl. Red sat opposite me, gazing across the large slab of the wooden table with his little piggy eyes. He was puffing as he sat. I noticed he had porridge upon his chin. Mother loomed up behind him.

'Egg?'

She extended a white, perfectly oval, shelled egg towards me. It quivered on the end of her spoon. The sight of it made me sick. I could imagine the fluid, running yolk exploding in a mass of juicy yellow against my plate, the sickening smoothness of the white being sliced open, the remnants of shell in splinters upon the porcelain.

'No thanks,' I said.

She looked mildly offended, or concerned, I wasn't sure which, but then put the egg back in the pot, poured herself a cup of coffee and buttered a piece of toast.

Having eaten enough porridge to satisfy Red, I slipped up to my bedroom and changed into my hippest new street gear. All my friends were jealous of my attire, 'cause it was the best in town. I had promised to nick Timmo a pair of jeans this morning before we met for lunch at the Big Girl's Arms. In exchange for the new wardrobe item, he had promised to listen to a second instalment of the circus/housewife novel. Buckell didn't know the first thing about either literature or housewives, and Larkin had a tendency to get too emotive on me, particularly when I got on to describing the activities of Carry at the circus and we'd all been knocking them back since three in the afternoon.

Buckell's problem was that he didn't see how a lower middle-class lad with a BA could get inside the head of a suburban woman. I told him it all came through acute observation and getting the right angle on things. Of course I considered myself the possessor of a soaring talent. Buckell said this was all pig's arse, and that if Willy was let loose with a word processor he'd come up with more interesting sentence combinations than I did. Poor, poor Buckell. You green-eyed monster, Buckell, I said to him, you poor old green-eyed beast. Just because I was capable of producing work of broad-based appeal. Buckell has an interesting and informative way of spouting the latest ideas on black holes and unified and super-string theories when nobody is listening. Like in a pub or a bar, when everybody is starting to sink a few gold ones and nobody really cares about anything much other than guessing the colour of the underpants of the girl at the next table.

So I had settled on Timmo for an audience. He was null enough to agree that my manuscript was of a superior kind and quality. Especially when I was sitting across the table from him with a pair of flash pants burning a hole in their own brown paper bag. Flash pants just like all the girls want their boys to be seen in. So here we were, the two of us in the Big Girl's Arms, me with the pants still sizzling under my armpit, crisping up in their brown paper bag. We called the barlady to bring us on over a pint each, and Timmo got himself a luke-warm steak and cheese pie. The last thing I wanted was for Timmo to lie to save my feelings. I wanted an honest opinion. Naturally, as I started to read, I was a little nervous, but with Timmo's encouragement I found that the voice came very naturally to me, and the words began to just sing themselves off the page.

'My dearest Caroline,
I am slowly coming to terms with your escape. This has been a slow and strenuous process for me, Carry, so please – do not take it lightly. I have passed through the denial stage, and am now on to grieving. Soon I shall be angry, and then I shall realise that I am well on

the way to good health. Your departure from the neighbourhood has left a stale fishy taste in my mouth, which I do not think can be entirely attributed to the eel pie. Oh, I hear your smutty snickers. Do not think I do not hear your voice travelling the miles. Sound waves are remarkable things, Carry, and they behave particularly peculiarly in the suburbs, where the air is denser. This town is not a vacuum, my dear, not silent like that. I can hear the homosexual couple who own the corner dairy carrying on and fighting late into the night. They are an odd pair. I feel they look at me as though I am slightly odd, especially of late. Gary says it's just my mind playing tricks, but I wouldn't be so sure now. The daughter of one of them has just had a terrible accident and is in a full-body cast behind the counter. God knows why she isn't tucked up away in bed. If the pair were especially busy, I could probably arrange to have Meals On Wheels brought to her door. I could deliver it myself. In fact, Carry, I believe I shall make that my good deed for the day. Back soon.

I have returned from the corner dairy to find the house in a complete shambles. The young daughter has refused my offer for Meals On Wheels, for the time being anyway. But, oh!, the house has been attacked by some man in a black balaclava. Or perhaps I accidentally left the three dining room windows open, causing books and papers to fling themselves about the room and a pane to shatter. The thought of an unwanted guest is almost more than I can bear.

I sat down, Carry, with a letter from my Eye. A fresh item, only just arrived in the box, buried beneath a pile of coupon booklets and Neighbourhood Watch pamphlets. Don't get it into your head that I sit and wait for news of you, as if waiting for a telephone call. I am rushed off my feet most of the time. It's difficult to turn down social offers, being such an upstanding pillar of the community.

Today I had my hair cut.

I shall transcribe this letter to you, Carry, for fear that you get a little too fancy-free on us. I feel that if I can give you an objective outside view of your behaviour you will come around to see sense. I shall never give up hope, Carry, hope that you will one day return to take up your proper position at the head of the family nest.

The circus crew appear to become fully animated after each night's show. Festivities and general debauchery carry on into the early morning hours. After the last act, the tent is swept out by the 'magician' and his blonde counterpart. The circus folk then gather in a circle, and consume large amounts of food and alcoholic beverages. The case appears to have developed an addiction to vodka. I have included an account of a story told one night by a Russian circus fellow, calling himself after Russia's greatest lover, Rasputin. A fire-eater by trade, he told the story to his fellows whilst working his way through a bottle of white liquor of unspecified substance. I have relayed this story to you, as a client, in order to demonstrate the fanciful and childish natures of these beastly circus folk. It is again recommended that you take action and attempt to persuade the case to return to her rightful neighbourhood. Remember – the law is on your side.

Here, then, is the tale as 'Rasputin' has told it, recorded rather inaccurately on my portable stereo, relayed through the white static of radio waves.

No winter season is crueller than that encountered by the Russian traveller. The whole world seems altered by the snow. The landscape is bleached, and damaging to the eye. It is Christmas every day. The statues wait with arms outstretched for the parcels which never arrive. The only sound is the howl of the predator. Which is the waltz chiming forth from the brass of the band. Which is also the clink of your neighbour clashing his glass to his plate. This is what it is to be a guest in a foreign land; a diplomat.

The orchestra is composed of wind-up toys, hired out for the occasion. A tin boy picks at the strings of a mandolin, a wooden man beats out the time on a tin drum.

Nobody hears the wolf at the door. His cry is drowned in the two-four rhythm and the stomping of black heels. The bride is immaculate in her mother's wedding dress. She glides across the dance floor with her groom as if in a slow-motion movie, her feet not seeming to touch the floor. How she has planned this day: the cake, the vodka, the sleigh ride home.

The guests grow weary as the night draws on. A small girl sleeps curled up in the corner, in front of the fire, her ribboned hair falling over her face. The bride dances on, oblivious to the air of fatigue which pervades the ballroom. The ice forms on the window panes as the predator circles, pawing the snow which encrusts the outside of the mansion, searching for a way in. Howling inconsolably, he is appetite incarnate. He cannot remember his last meal; the black pit of his stomach has become the black hole of his mind.

In through the lighted window the groom devours the last of the wedding cake. The wolf waits and watches. Finally, the last song is played, the toy orchestra pack their instruments away and the guests make ready to leave. The front door of the palace creaks on its heavy iron hinge and the groom steps out into the snow. The horses are saddled and made ready, their breath issuing out before them in fine shots of steam. They shudder with the weight of the carriage and the constriction of the blinkers. The wolf will content himself with nothing less than virgin blood. The taste of baby's wedding gown will be as sugar to his tongue. One of his kindred howls from over the ice plateau; this beast does not call back, but rather slinks himself behind an empty vodka crate, haunches bristling. The saliva drips from his grisly chops.

The radiant bride is talking to a friend of Poppa's, a consul, who extends his heart-felt congratulations to the couple. He shows her to the door, where her love lies waiting in a stupor. Oh Vladimir! You have never been able to handle your vodka. See! He's so cold, his hands are turning purple. Here. Let me remove my veil and cover him in the soft billow of the white material. The consul helps the bride to wrap her husband. But still he shivers. I must cover him with my coat, my polar bear fur. Take my coat for yourself, says the consul, the colour brings out the whites of your lovely eyes. The bride blushes. We must carry him to the carriage, then return to show the others the way.

The wolf strains against himself as the white figure is dragged across the snow, then left alone in the carriage. Dobbyn screams as the carnivore streaks across the ice. My nearby ravine, oh!, my secret lair. Here I have lain the skeletons of seventy-seven wedding guests.

A bloody trail follows the tracks of the wolf. Upstairs, in the palace, the bride stands before the looking glass, fingering the empty vial of arsenic trioxide. The consul ravishes her for the third time that day, then proposes marriage on bended knee.

Such stories as the above are told late into the evening, often by the same chap, the Russian. His stories grow increasingly lewd as the night progresses and he consumes his vodka. He is subject to any amount of abuse from his fellow circus members, but appears mostly oblivious to the onslaught, both verbal and fruitage. This story being told on the sixth night of the Wainui performances, the tent was packed away afterwards and stored inside one of the larger caravans. Tomorrow the circus will be beginning its journey northwards. I have enclosed a map of the proposed route, and urge you to contact the police at the second location (circled in red ink). Please help us all to enforce the law and make this a better country. This circus seems more than mere entertainment.

Report complete.

Oh my Carry! I do hope you do not listen to these ridiculous Russian tales too often. I will send with this letter a copy of the Gideon's Bible, so that you may repay this Russian gentleman with a dose of sound Christianity. For a small quote, temperate and pleasing to the senses, may I recommend Job 19:2. We are all born weak and helpless, Carry, and must turn to the Lord for support and guidance. I pray for you every night, Carry, kneeling down by your goldfish bowl, and watching the flecks of Fisho filter slowly down through the currents. You are as a crumb of Fisho, my Carry, adrift on an endless fishbowl of an ocean. But I trust that you will soon realise your true home is not among the waves, nor in the ocean depths, but back here with us in the Street. I write to you now as your one touchstone of reality.

Gary sends his sickly regards, and begs you to come back to him, if only for the children's sake. He has seen a doctor regarding the impotence and the bowel disorder, and says that Mr Willy has regained his former altitudinal ability. Please return to the Street.

Your loving fisherman,
P. Gluckendown'

Timmo was lying face down in a small puddle of beer. I shook his shoulders briefly. He jerked up, and surveyed the bar before spitting into his empty beer glass.

'That was amazing. I thought the bit about the girls was special, really special. And the bit about the white lines. Going the wrong way. And the little bugs getting their bodies splattered open. That's real nice. Blood and gore. Oi! You should think about going into films, bud. With that Tarantula bloke. The one that did *Arachnophobia*.'

'Timmo, what I have just presented to you is a sensitive and elegant portrait of a woman in the grips of a slow and stealthy mental decline. Have you grasped that? These reports are so badly written, my boy, that they couldn't possibly be by a real private Eye. Stories by a Russian named Rasputin? Crap fairytales rehashed in a most appalling manner, just conveniently relayed via a report, via a tape recording? It's imagination, mate, and that's the whole point. Loss of cerebral control, inability to differentiate between reality and fantasy, the whole kabutz, sunshine. Have you cleaned out your earholes? This is not just slapstick, my son, this is . . . this is *pastiche* . . . this is . . . a carefully orchestrated piece, moving dedicatedly inwards, just *like* . . . ' (and here I lowered the pitch of my voice whilst raising the volume so as to give the effect of a master of his works) ' . . . *a set of Chinese boxes*.'

Pause. Sip pint. Smack lips. Inhale.

'Have you comprehended that, you ignorant numbskull? You will notice that I, like God, stay above and behind my creation, paring my fingernails out of existence.' I paused, not exactly sure that I had got the quotation quite right. 'Paring my fingernails out of existence. Yes, that's it. Paring them down to the stubby and tortured and bleeding flesh. Yet you'll find no specks of cuticle present in my work. Ah no, you'll find no stench of Jimmy in these texts. I have observed the mind of the bourgeois, my boy, and I *know* about suburban women. What exactly would an oaf like you hope to know about suburban neurosis, Timmo? I, Timmo, *I* have observed the best ovaries of my generation addling the best minds. I wish to show the hormonal difficulties, the prison house that is the female body. The longing, and oh, Timmo, how ardent that longing, that aching burning feverish desire . . .' (here I added a small pause, for effect, and also to allow me to remember the object of the longing) ' . . . for *freedom,* Timmo, oh, for freedom. I wish to save the female from her own body, from her own *mind,* from the twin prison houses of mind and body. The true essence of a woman, oh my son, is a vapourish and ethereal spirit. A spirit with the scent of rose petal and dew . . .'

'Can I have my jeans now?'

' . . . where the raven lights upon a high wire. There is woman. Where the frost first touches the green grass in winter. There is woman. Where the candle gutters and dies. There is woman.'

'Oh shit. You got red. Maroon's not groovy, man . . . maroon's just not where it's at.'

'The shape, Timmo, the white shape which hovers in periphery, or flits as a ballerina on the back of closed eyelids. That, my young friend, is woman.'

I sat savouring the last chimes of my voice ringing out around the recently vacated bar. I felt myself to be the genius of my age. For truly, to understand and to show sensitivity towards both the sexes was the art of any poet of integrity.

Still high on the fumes of my own vocality, I shouted to the barmaid to bring over another couple of pints. Shit she had an arse and a half. I made sure that Timmo had his favourite Guinness, so as to console him for the colour of the denim jeans. The blue jeans had been too far towards the rear of the shop, where the shop assistant lurked like a large and predatory Great White, so I had swiped a maroon pair from the front shelves and beat it on out of there.

We had only taken a few short sips of our new ales when Buckell made his fetid appearance.

'Boys,' he nodded briefly towards us both, then sat his satchel down upon the seat next to mine.

'Any new thoughts on black holes to share with us today, Bucko?'

'Call me that one more time, Jimmy boy, and you'll be tasting the fresh suds of the toilet bowl.'

'Any new thoughts on black holes to share with us today, Bucko?'

'Listen very closely and don't say a word. I have just suffered through five hours of mind-numbingly boring lectures, and I don't need you saying my name like that. You got it?'

I could hear the town clock chiming six. The cracked mirror on the opposite wall shone back several fragmented selves. I had to be getting home. I stood up and excused myself to the boys, apologising profusely to Timmo for the faulty denim colouring.

'You'll be having something blue knocking on your door one day soon, anyway, if you carry on at this rate, boyo.'

Buckell's Pa was a merchant banker, and his mother was a doctor. He had all the blue denim he wanted. Buckell had never been to my house. It wasn't that I was ashamed, or anything like that, not like my folks thought, that I was ashamed of Willy or something. 'Cause I wasn't. I just didn't think that it was right and fitting that an up-and-coming first-rate novelist be seen to be living with his folks. I never lied about it. I just dodged and dived around the truth, in order to save all parties concerned a good deal of embarrassment.

We arranged to meet same time, same place, tomorrow.

I scooped my manuscript out from where it lay sodden in a pool of beer and walked out through the wooden doorframe and into the deserted street. I walked home via the river, passing the museum of natural history, and the art gallery with its black bricks and white turrets. I crossed the bridge that ran above the trains, pausing at mid-way to listen to the bells chiming from the crossing in the distance, listening for the fall of the barriers. Turning into my own street, I saw that nothing was moving.

I saw my own home.

The place was lit up like a whorehouse, every room radiating a yellow glare out into the street. A police car was pulled up outside the front porch, lights flickering silently upon the roof. I held my breath, as though about to dive under water, crossed the porch and entered the front room.

My idiot brother lay swollen and blue upon the front room floor.

III

PATRICIA

Dear Carry,
How I hate to write. But I must tell you the truth. The worst has happened. I hope you are sitting down with a stiff gin. I am. Your beautiful three goldfish are now two goldfish. Yes, Caroline, I am afraid that I was so concerned with locking the house properly this morning, after my recent burglary, that I quite forgot to put Tiddles outside. I came home to find the old puss perched over the fish bowl, quite terrifying the two survivors. A small golden fin lay upon the dresser. What can I say? I shall do my best to replace the poor tyke with a simulacrum, but I guess that we shall always know in our hearts that the thing is a fake. I hope I have not spoiled your night's performance in telling you this. Then again, it takes a fair bit to break *your* stride, doesn't it?

Well, that's the grisly stuff over with. The bright news is that the young daughter of the dairy homosexual has accepted my offer to provide her with Meals On Wheels, and we have struck up quite a friendship. Poor dear, it can't be easy for her, what with her father suddenly up and running away with the managing director of his company and the two of them buying a small corner shop in the suburbs. I expect she finds it a frightful bore after the big city. That was one of your major complaints, wasn't it? 'Stifling' was the word I believe you were fond of. I always say it's up to the individual to make their own fun. Thank the Lord you had all limbs functioning, Caro, or you would have been at quite a loss as to what to do with yourself during all those long hours between the dinner table and the bedroom. As it was, you took up dance and yoga. I took up cleaning.

As young Jasmine says, there is only so much fun to be had in a full-body cast. She is wheeled into the shop every morning to chat to the customers as they dash in to grab the morning paper and a pint of milk. Really, it is quite bizarre. She looks a bit like a milk bottle herself, all bandaged up in white. She has to be spoon-fed, and even then quite often chokes, as swallowing whilst vertical is no easy feat. Though I hear that you manage it quite well. I mean no smut, only that my latest Eye Report informs me that you skull vodka whilst lying in bed at night. If this is true, then I fear you are on the downward spiral. Beware the drink! Each bottle contains a tiny winged demon, invisible to the naked eye.

Do you have a lover? Gary flashes past my dining room window every day on the way to the office. He is badly in need of a haircut, so I shall give him a trim after dinner tonight. I have been encouraging him to take up squash but he says he is too embarrassed to be seen in shorts. I told him to play in tracksuit pants. I fear he may be taking a fancy to the lady-head of the new family who has just moved in across the road at number 108. He was over there to borrow the lawn-mower last night. She is a dancer, and has an uncouth habit of prancing around the place in a tight black leotard with not even a jersey over the top. It's quite disgusting, such an open display of curves. She looks like your type. I shall warn him away from her when he comes over for eel pie leftovers tonight. Must dash, got a thousand appointments,

Patricia

Dearest Caro,
I warned Gary about Mrs Tartick. He laughed it off, and said that she didn't tickle his fancy. She looks like the tickling type to me. What example is she to her two young children? It is only fortunate that they have a neighbour like myself to provide the soft wings of maternity. I shall knit them jumpers for the winter. Red for the girl and navy blue for the boy. I have started some fairisle socks for Jasmine, the young girl at the dairy. I have had to make them XOS so they will fit over the plaster. She says that her feet don't get cold, but I suspect she is just being a martyr. She is a cheerful wee sparrow, considering the circumstances, but remains strangely quiet as to her accident, and so I do not press her for details. She will open up in her own good time, I suspect.

Well, Gary came over for tea, as planned, and once the topic of Mrs Tartick was out of the way, we had a jolly old time. My pies are doing wonders for his complexion. He has never looked so flushed and cheerful. He has talked me into going to his staff do with him next Friday night. Oh course, I was fairly hesitant, but he twisted my elbow. I didn't want the poor dear to look as if he had no partner. Must dash. Finish tomorrow.

Today I bought some new diamante earrings for the staff do tonight. Quite exciting. They sparkle most prettily. I imagine they are somewhat similar to the glitz and glitter which decorate your costume, although a little more classy. I have not heard from my Eye Reporter for quite some time, but shall be expecting something within the next day or two.

My Eye Reporter is a master of invisibility. I only work with the best, Carry, you know that. I am tempted to tell Gary about the Eye I keep on you, but

I fear he is immersed in the denial stage, and is still unwilling to accept not only that you have run away but that you have also left him to become part of a circus troop. When I feel he is ready to accept the fact of your departure and whorish profession, I shall show him the back catalogue of reports. Until then, only I shall know of your new vocation. It amazes me, Carry. I shudder to think how you have justified your actions to yourself. I suppose you have quite a different perspective on this whole thing, a different tilt of the head or squinting of the eyelids. The human memory gorges itself on shades of lie and tricks of light. I have been praying day and night that the Lord should send me some sign of you. Must go and iron an outfit fit for the accounting do. Something in plain black, to set off the diamante earrings and underplay my rump.

Hope to hear of you soon,

Patricia Gluckendown

My dearest Carry,
I am nursing a slight headache. I am afraid I got a bit carried away on the old gin and tonics, and may have let something slip about my correspondence with the Eye. I am not sure whether I was chatting to Gary, or one of his workmates. Mr Blank was rather blurry, but I do recall flashes of a red and grey diagonally striped tie over a navy blue shirt. I do hope it wasn't Gary, for I fear he may split in two and lie fragmented upon the floor if he is forced to face the truth of the situation. I feel I may have made rather a fool of myself. I don't much feel like answering the door, nor the telephone, and think that I might just lie in bed all day with a cold pack of Wattie's peas upon my forehead and ponder the latest report. I shall transcribe it for you here, and add my advice about all matters as I see fit, despite the team of mountaineers ice-picking at my temples.

Today I witnessed the circus master in action. He is an obese bald man, sporting a ginger beard. His manner towards the circus crew is almost tyrannical. The crew appear to take great delight in mocking and impersonating him. He is the only member of the team not to take part in the post-show festivities. Rasputin's stories grow more fanciful by the night. I relay for you, here again, a tale I recorded whilst crouched in the corner of the tent.

In the summer months the sun hardly seems to set. The shadow of the palace grows in length until it might appear to stretch to the far wall. The palace wall sits forty foot wide and eighty foot high, impassable to all travellers. The wall, designed to keep the inside in and the outside out, has no door. Inside the wall are no thorny thickets; only freshly clipped grass lies felled upon the lawn. The royalty are self-sufficient inbreds.

The King sits in the parlour, gloating over the golden

bird he has in the wicker cage. A yellow ice carving, the note still fresh in its throat. If only the cage were also golden. Ah well, such is the price of insulation. One must content oneself with wicker for the time being. The Queen sits also, rubbing herself with essential oils to eliminate any odours. Even within the wall one has entertaining to do, and an orderly self to present. And is Petal preparing herself for the night's entertainment?

At the top of a long golden stair, the princess sits in the highest room of the turret. What fun is there in flirtation, when all the men are one's cousins? My children will be mutants. We shall become diseased and die. It is unholy to breed in such a manner. We shall refuse to couple, and become extinct. Petal reaches into a small woven bag tied around her waist, draws out Eleanor's red marble and fondles it between her fingers. When Eleanor, the servant-girl, died, this was the only thing we left unburied.

The squeals of Porky being slaughtered rise up to the window. Life is short, little piggy, and I must escape. Tonight I shall dance again, and hope that he will see me. The sun must eventually go down. After the celebrations, it will be night again. We cannot have this yellow light for two hundred hours every week. The dinner gong is chiming.

There are no clocks in the palace. All inhabitants work according to the King's whim. The King is hungry; chime the gong and we shall eat. If the turkey has been waiting for two hours, we shall eat it cold. A basted wing for Petal? We shall play cards all day if we wish; all day we shall admire the golden bird and the iron note. Do you remember when it once sang silver? Here, we have it recorded, so let's spin the disc and dance to its pretty tune.

But, Pappa, we dance every night. I am so tired,

see, I have black circles around my eyes. We always dance the same dance. I am always waltzing with my cousins. I am so tired. May I be excused?

But my child, you have hardly touched your dinner!

Let me rest. I shall join tomorrow's lunchtime festivities with a joyful heart.

Ask your mother.

The princess retires to her bedroom.

Now I must learn to wait. When the light fades from yellow through red to dark blue, then he will see me again. I have locked my own room, and have the only key in my small bag with my red marble. I shall scale the building, then maybe he will fetch white horses and come for me tomorrow. I hope that it will be night, before I become too old to be taken. It has occurred to me that I may be in the land of the citroens, where the sun never sets. Night will never fall in the land of the lemon trees.

The recorded bird chirps on in the palace ballroom.

From my window I can see Eleanor's grave. We buried her with the rest of the marbles. I am waiting. The sun is not moving. The record is still spinning. When will I hear the next gong? The sky is not even orange. Is he waiting on the far side of the wall?

Mamma's laugh floats up the golden staircase. She is dancing with the gardener, who picks her fresh pink roses from the palace garden every morning. The King is finishing off the turkey. The gong sounds. Darkness.

Petal rises from the bed, and picks her way down the golden staircase to the first landing. From there she scales the side of the palace and alights softly upon the marshy ground. The palace wall is in darkness now, but knowing the places for small hands and feet, she scrambles up the crumbling brick. She is dancing on the wall, all over the wall now. Oh Pappa, if you only knew why I was so tired every evening. And faster, and the sky is spinning, and the earth falls away into the sky and becomes the sky and . . .

A shrill whistle comes from the forest. He is watching. He must be watching, he said he would be. For the last seven nights he has stood in the shadows of the bushes, outside the wall. There is no way inside. The princess dances closer to the edge. Oh, take care in your delicate red slippers! The prince licks his lips and swings his tail. He lets out another whistle and then a small howl. The princess freezes, one toe poised over the precipice. There are dogs! Are they Pappa's hounds? Are they watchdogs? The prince howls again, then pads across the pine needles to the wall. The moonlight lights up his muzzle, the princess screams and falls, falls over the edge of the wall, into the waiting arms of the beast.

Ah Petal, ah Beauty! Now your father has lost you. I shall take you to my chamber, and dress you in fine linen. I shall stand you in my mirrored room, and make of you a toy.

The wolf sinks his fangs into the virgin neck of the melted princess.

What's this? No blood!

This girl is bleeding glass, not fluid. The princess grasps her red marble all the more tightly. Blood drips from the glass surface of the handmade stone as the beast withdraws a sliver of mirror from his lip. How can she be made of mirrors? The blood from the marble is leaking, nay, flooding through the woven bag, and staining the paw of the wolf. The wolf tears open the lower arm of the princess. Glass splinters tinkle on to the floor, the sound of the smashing of vodka glasses. Eleanor's marble spurts blood like a severed artery, simulating the gush which comes from the mouth of the beast. He howls. My own blood! I have loved a woman of glass. My little ivory tower! The beast streaks back to his castle, wounded mouth now silent.

Petal stands amongst a pool of congealing blood, upon which splinters of glass shimmer and fade in the light of the moon. Her shadow stretches out like a beast before her as she stalks towards the edge of the vast black forest.

I relay these stories to you, as I fear they may be distorting the mind of the case. She seems to be taking the fanciful fairy tales to heart, and has been seen to stand up and applaud drunkenly at the outcomes. She has dyed her hair a shocking shade of yellow, and wears little other than a loose piece of material knotted at the waist, and a tatty singlet during the day. I have noticed that she has made progressions from the tight-rope, and now flies quite regularly upon the trapezes. I feel I may not have adequately stressed the immediate danger which this woman is in. She risks life and limb nightly. She performs without a safety net. I cannot risk exposing myself to her, and am subsequently in no position to reproach or reprimand her. I feel she is not thinking rationally, for certainly a good deal of her behaviour is of the agitated and restless variety. Please contact the police a.s.a.p. so that the case may be saved from herself.
End report.

You see the situation you have put me in. I cannot tell *anybody* about you, let alone the police. I am afraid they will think I am stark raving bonkers, Carry, for believing that you are now with the travelling circus. All I can do is advise you, as one good Christian to . . . well, one good Christian to one circus performer, to steer clear of those Russian types. I've seen their sort, drunkenly stalking the streets having just arrived in on the fishing boats, all gold teeth and American dollars. They're all full of the same old rubbish. All men are, Carry. Of course, my Bert wasn't like that, but then he wasn't like most men in a lot of ways.

I fear I may have made quite a spectacle of myself last night. To start with, I have never felt myself to be much of the belle of the ball type, and with all these young office-girl types around, I felt quite out of place. I asked one pretty young blonde thing if she wouldn't mind popping over to ask her boss (Gary) to introduce me, as I had arrived alone. (Gary had left without me, forgetful old thing, so I had made my own way there.) I asked her if she wouldn't mind being a good little secretary and fetching me one of those scrumptious-looking shrimp cocktails while she was at it. Well, she did as I asked, Caroline, and she came back with the cocktail and Gary, who then introduced her as his boss. I swear to our Father in heaven, I blushed the colour of the drink in my hand. Of course she had to gloat about it then, didn't she, oh yes, she'd had her little victory. Smarmy tart. I wasn't about to let her get the better of me, oh no, we'd see who could lead the men around by the necktie. So I drank, Carry. I am ashamed to say that I was but a limp puppet beneath the command of the demon of shrimp cocktails. I drank for the both of us, Caro; I drank for the three of us, you, me and Bertie; I drank for the Street. Caroline, I drank for my country.

I do seem to recall telling the cheap blonde hussy who reported to run the place that I bet she couldn't organise a piss-up in a brewery, and that I knew exactly how she had won her way to the top. I believe I may have mentioned a certain golden prize. I think she may then have said that she'd actually organised the staff do that night, including the beverages, and that if I thought *that* way I could just (go away) and who in (the infernal regions) had brought me along anyway.

Gary was nowhere to be seen by this stage of the action. I think he might have gone home inexplicably early. After the hussy incident, I recall a sort of pinky shrimp-flavoured haze and then the blinding white flash of the photocopier. Oh, my dear heart, but I think I may have photocopied the outline of my derrière and handed it out free-of-charge to all those present. And after that, well, flashes of porcelain, Caroline, water flushing, toilet paper, and shrimps, shrimps, shrimps. I shall never eat seafood again. Oh Caroline, my peas are becoming mushy and disintegrating slightly. I shall have to go to the refrigerator to search for a frozen meatpack with which to nurse my pounding temples.

For now I shall remain your loving and nauseous friend,

Patricia Gluckendown

Oh my dear Caroline,
Gary has just paid me a visit, and seems to think I am the laughing stock of the office. Of course, he said that all the staff are laughing *with* me rather than at me. He has quite allayed all my irrational fears of having made a complete idiot of myself in a public place. I feel safe and secure in accepting the invitation from the office staff to attend the next Christmas do. The invitation quite oddly stated to bring an entertainment. I am not sure what was meant by that, so shall just bring myself. He is a wonderful man, your husband, truly wonderful. Why on earth would you leave such a man? I never dreamed of leaving Bertie, not even when his problem worsened in his later years. I believe that the separate beds held our marriage together. Of course we had our rough times: when we found we were unable to have children, when Bertie went on that wee holiday to the Bahamas with that tart from across the road. Still, I guess he did need the break. Such a shame that the young thing was ravaged by a man-eating shark whilst snorkelling and admiring the tropical fish darting amongst the delicate pink coral. At least, that's what I believe happened to her. Bertie told me she had moved south and taken a job in a bank, but that doesn't account for the excessively fishy odour lingering around his beach togs. Bertie's story was just Bertie being modest, and not wanting to boast about the way in which he had wrestled the shark in an attempt to save the young twit. A true soldier he was, our Bertie, one of God's little army. I believe our Gary would wrestle a shark for *you*, Caroline. Certainly, I have seen him have an affectionate play in the goldfish bowl.

Oh, yes! The new fish is settling in well. I have named her. I hope you don't mind. Yes, I have named her Moray, in the expectation that she will one day grow to match the destiny her name holds for her. She flits about the bowl and looks quite contented. When she grows a little bigger, I shall take her as a gift to the poor girl at the corner dairy, and buy you a replacement. Jasmine has been looking a touch despondent lately, and I fear that she is feeling just a little cooped up. After all, life cannot be easy in a full-body plaster cast. I hold out hope that she will one day tell me the circumstances surrounding her accident. As I hope that you will return home.

Did I mention that Gary left the staff do early? Yes, and looking slightly desperate. Despite his macho-man accountant-type appearance, I fear he is not able to fend for himself at all well. Living on one's own is not healthy for the psyche. Of course, there are the children, but how much help can they really be? Oh, I know they're lovely things, but in many ways they are more liability than asset. I feel blessed that I never had any of my own.

I must go and visit my little friend at the corner store.

Your loving friend,
Patricia

Caro,
I have just been across to the corner dairy, to see the young invalid. We have built up quite a rapport now. I dare say she begins to think of me as a substitute mother.

So I felt quite at ease to bring up the subject of her accident. I was not burning with curiosity. I just thought it might be healthy for her to get it off her chest. I handed her Moray in a bag, so she might feel that I was willing to absorb some of the pain of her experience. Through gifts and sundry tokens, but also, as every Christian knows, through being a Good Ear.

The poor girl talked in puffs and monosyllabic grunts, but I think I may have discerned the general gist of the story. I believe a car was involved; yes, a flaming car. Also, she motioned some sort of large and fiery accident. Eventually we got things down to me play-acting and the girl nodding or shaking her head in agreement or disagreement with what I was acting out. I haven't had so much fun since the staff do.

I pulled out a packet of Jaffas from behind the counter, and we mutually agreed that they should be the car. I drove the Jaffas at high speed along the edge of the counter, then plummeted them over the side. She shook her head furiously. I was not easily off-put. I shook four Jaffas out of the packet and drew faces on each of them. She shook again and held up three fingers. I ate one of the figures. I then poured a small bottle of vanilla essence down the 'throat' of one of my Jaffa characters. She nodded again, and looked away. You will understand, Caroline, how painful this was for the both of us. But sometimes the hurt is like a sticking plaster, and you must jerk it off, as quickly as possible. Then the true wound may heal. My mother told me that.

My friend gazed wistfully at Moray swimming free

in his plastic bag. I set up the Jaffas packet at one end of the counter for another go. She cried out, and shook her head before I reached the edge. I admit I was a little mystified for a moment, so I then held the car suspended in mid-air and dropped it. Her head gave a small half-nod. I gazed around the shelves as I thought. Weetbix, canned tuna, instant coffee in a glazed packet, toilet rolls, tinned beetroot, cigarette papers, razor blades, pencil sharpeners, pencils, rubbers, rulers. Rulers! Yes, a ruler had been involved. Now I was hot on the scent. Moray flicked his tail twice.

'Was a ruler involved?' I asked as sensitively as possible.

She then looked at me as if I was a little odd.

I took the ruler from the shelf, and placed one end of it upon the front counter, fetched the ladder from the back of the shop, and rested the other end of the ruler upon that. I drove the car crazily around the counter, then slowed down to take it up on to the ruler. She was nodding furiously. Then, not quite half-way across the ruler, I dropped Jaffa down over the edge, so that she spilled a violent stream of orange sweeties as she fell. Oh, it was quite beautiful, Caroline, just the sort of arty-farty thing that you used to go in for.

Bending over, I picked up three of the Jaffas from the floor. I held one out, and said, 'You.' She nodded. I placed it gently in my mouth. Jaffas have always been my soft spot. I held out another Jaffa and said, 'Driver.' Then, 'Option One', and I danced the Jaffa happily around the counter. She shook her head. I took out a packet of matches from behind the glass and laid a small white cross over the Jaffa. She nodded. I was about to do the same with the second Jaffa, when one of the homosexuals returned from walking the dog.

'Minding shop for us, Patricia?' he inquired, surveying the contents of the car spilled upon the floor.

'Yes,' I said, 'just keeping the children entertained.'

'Can I trust you here for another five minutes? I've got some bills to fix up out the back.'

'Yes. We were just climaxing.'

He looked at me strangely, then went out the back. Oh, they're odd types, these homosexuals. They tend to be confused, not only in their sexuality, but also in their day-to-day living. It's against nature, it is, using the old back passage in a way it was never intended to be used. God will get them all in the end. Divine Justice.

My girl was starting to cry now, so I left off the third passenger for the moment and dangled Moray in front of her face for a bit, then popped a few Jaffas into her mouth. She swallowed, then looked as if she might throw up or choke. There was a small Jaffa-sized lump in the middle of her windpipe. It was in this sort of atmosphere that I felt the trust necessary to announce my plans for the circus.

So I started off at the beginning, so as to give her the whole story. I said about you, and how you'd lived on the Street, though were always something of the outrageous type, then I said how you'd run away to the circus. She was very quiet, then, and didn't make so much as a grunt. I said how you lived, travelling about with the dwarfs, and Buffo the clown, and Rasputin, and how tales from Russia were told, and I mentioned a bit about the princess and then about the bride, and how you swung high on the trapezes and you had at least thirty different costumes, all sequined and feathered, and how you all bathed in the town rivers, how you were soon to go overseas, but I was going to find you soon, with the aid of . . .

And she started to scream and scream. I thought my eardrums might split.

She had a fine set of lungs on her, I'll say that. She hollered and she hollered, and I hadn't even got on to the bit about meeting Steven in the park. Her father's partner came rushing into the dairy and glared at me like I was somehow responsible.

The screaming must have burst Moray's bag, for he lay flapping and gasping upon the floor, water gushing over the counter and coating the passengers with a fine spray. She was still screaming, increasing in both volume and pitch with every second that passed. I bolted for the door, leaving Moray still writhing and wriggling, God save his little soul.

I locked the front door behind me, and began this letter to you. I hope you'll understand. I never meant any harm. I just thought it would be nice if I shared something of my personal life in exchange for all that she had told me about the crash. I must go, I have developed a frightful headache.

Your friend,
Patricia Gluckendown

Dear Carry,
On the way back from the store I took a walk through the park, and the oddest thing happened. The most charming man introduced himself to me, and stated that he had heard all about my predicament. When I asked what predicament he could possibly mean, he behaved most mysteriously, and simply said that he should like to join me for a cup of tea and a biscuit, so as to discuss the matter. Of course, I was more than a little hesitant at being approached by such a stranger. He was a dark man of average height, wearing a blue accountant's suit with narrow stripes on it. From a distance he looked quite dashing, but as I got closer I saw how haggard he really was. His eyes had prominent crows' feet protruding from the edges, and his mouth had a decidedly beak-like feel to it. Don't ask me to explain this, Caroline, but there was something very other-worldly about this man.

I suggested we go back to my place for a cuppa, and he agreed. The tulips in the park looked more blood-red than ever, Caro, and the leaves were all in their proper places, green on the trees, not red and brown and chasing each other across the floor of the park. I have not been to this park for quite a while. I usually come at night-time, when I circle the shadows of the elms in the dark and can get a full view of the stars. So we walked home in silence, me struggling to keep pace with his larger stride. I swear, the whole neighbourhood looked quite different in the presence of this stranger. I hoped that Gary wasn't watching out his bedroom window on this early Sunday morning.

We arrived back at the old place, and I let him in. He said he knew about my friend who had run away to join the travelling circus, and that he fully intended to help me get in contact with her. I chastised him, and inquired as to how he had come across such confidential information, for after all, Carry, I have told nobody of your whereabouts. It was then that he produced a third letter from the Eye, claiming that it had been sent to his own address by mistake. My name had been on the envelope, so he had looked me up in the telephone book and found that I lived on the street below his. Naturally, I felt a little disconcerted when I learnt that he had been spying on me through his binoculars for the last three days. However, he turned out to be an amiable enough sort of chap, much like our Bertie in his younger days, although a good deal slimmer. He handed me the letter across the table and said that we should discuss getting in contact with you after I had read it.

I sat down to read the letter, which contained no real news, bar the fact that the circus had four more towns to perform in before leaving for Australia. The stranger pecked away at his seed biscuit, then put it down half finished on his plate. I encouraged him to have another, to have two more, but he politely refused, pleading lack of appetite. He is such a scarecrow of a man! When I had finished the latest report of the circus, I asked the stranger his name. He was slightly hesitant on the subject, but I eventually managed to pry a 'Steven' from his lips. Whether this is a last or a Christian name, I was unable to discern.

Steven lowered his eyelids, then reached across the table to grasp my hand between his larger, more powerful ones.

'Mrs Gluckendown . . . Patricia.' He paused. 'May I call you Patricia?'

My heart was beginning to do a quick little foxtrot, for it has been quite a while since my hand was grasped by a gentleman.

'Patricia, I believe I know the very circus where your

dear friend Tara is to be located.'

'Caro,' I quickly corrected.

'Yes, Caro.' He took a sip of his tea, then took another crumb off his biscuit. His nails were long and pointed, slightly reptilian. 'You see, my brother left for the same circus, this time last year.'

I emitted a small noise so as to signify shock. 'The same circus?'

'He had been leading a normal life as a gynaecologist, working down here at City Central. Then one morning I went in to see him at work, and they said he'd just vanished. Quite disappeared. Very odd. His workmates were most surprised that I hadn't read about it in the papers, and that I hadn't been contacted by the police. Nobody knew where he was. They suspected it had been just one vagina too many. Well, naturally, this all came as a terrible shock.'

Steven broke off, and shook his head in dismay. I didn't feel that I should push him for details, but rather let all the information come out in its own good time. He was clearly not fully recovered. Well, I of all people know how hard these things are to come to terms with. Still, life in the suburbs grinds on.

'Everybody presumed he'd left the country. Then I did a little research. Hired a detective to track him down. Turned out he'd left for the same circus your friend has. I didn't feel I could do anything about it at the time.' Steven gazed deep into my eyes. I felt as though I might drown in two black whirlpools. 'Together, Mrs Gluckendown . . . '

'Patricia.'

'Together, Patricia, I think we could retrieve our lost ones from the circus.'

'They are but sheep strayed from the fold, Steven . . . '

'Yes.'

We were silent for a moment, listening to the distant purr of traffic rising up from the motorway.

'We shall find them, Steven.'

'Yes, Patricia.'

We set off on a brief bumpy ride through the city in a taxi, then returned home and played a few rounds of chess. Steven began to outstay his welcome, and I grew tired. In order to rid myself of his presence, I found it necessary to surreptitiously drop a purple-striped tropical fish down the front of his shirt. This convinced him to take his leave. We agreed to set off for the circus a week from today, so as to allow time to tidy up our immediate affairs here. So, Caroline, we are off to find the circus. I shall be seeing you fairly soon, then. With Steven on my side, I hope we shall easily dissuade you from continuing on with this nonsense and bring you back to the fold. I have invited Steven to dinner in a few nights' time, so as to introduce him to Gary and so that we may announce our plans to an Official Outsider. I am quite excited about it all, and shall have to have a cup of tea and a lie-down so as not to get too frantic.

Your Guide In All Things,

P. Gluckendown

Dear Caroline,
I dreamed about the circus last night. It was very distorted. You see, Steven was all dressed up in this big black suit, like a raven, and I was dressed all in white. We found you bathing in the river. Then, that night, when we watched you perform, we thought it was so lovely we didn't want to come back home. We just stayed with you, travelling around and eating fresh grapes and watermelon every morning for breakfast. I dreamed that I was pouring vodka all over myself, and I awoke to find that I must have upset the fish bowl, and water and fish were all over my face.

Must go and prepare the lamb for Gary and Steven tonight.

P.G.

My dear friend Caroline,
I made a frightful mess at the dinner. You see, Steven didn't turn up, so I got a bit flustered and burnt the lamb. When Gary asked who Steven was, and why he wasn't there, I found myself rather hard-pushed to explain the whole situation. So I started with you. I told all. But oh my dear Caro, Gary is in a worse way than I thought. I feel that he is really very sick and may even need to be hospitalised. When I told him the truth concerning your whereabouts, he turned quite pale. He became most upset and told me that I had been acting rather peculiarly, and that he had heard about the dairy incident. I assured him that I was perfectly all right, and that he must worry only about his own health. I reassured him that you were healthy and well cared for, that the circus had unions to counteract the tyranny of the circus master. (Well, what else could I say? I had to tell him something.) Oh, Caroline, he has told himself a fanciful little story, some frightful thing about you going on a management training course to Australia, just for the month. I tried to put him straight and tell him, yes, you were intending to go to Australia, with the circus, in about a month, but that Steven and I were going in, like Christian crusaders, to stop you. Full chest armour, swords ablazing. He asked me again about Steven, and I told him of our meeting, of the common link we had, what with us each having a loved one run away to the circus. My Caro, and Steven's gyno. Gary did not look impressed, only rather tired and drawn, and said that he thought I might need a little holiday, somewhere in the country, with some friends of his. Forgive him, Caroline, he is still coming to terms with your departure.

He only picked at his lamb, so I ate my own dinner and then finished his off for him. He moaned that he didn't think I was eating properly, but I fear this was only a disguise for his own lack of respect for self and body. He asked me when I was next seeing Steven, and I replied, 'Why, tomorrow we're heading away together, to find Caroline. Steven has the circus tour etched on a papier maché map, so if we don't catch up with them in one centre, we can simply follow the trail north. We're quite prepared to go across the ocean to Australia if needs be. Caroline doesn't know what she's doing, Gary. She needs a good God-fearing mind to put some sense into her again. You know how one can be led astray by one's immediate environment.'

Gary left my house then, quite abruptly, although I ran after him with a couple of lamb chops wrapped up in a white napkin, lest he get hungry during the night and feel like a good gnaw. Ah well, when I bring you back, he shall see that I was only trying to tell him the truth. You shall confirm all my stories. Anyway, must go and pack, for tomorrow is the Big Day. Steven will be turning up on my front doorstep quite early, I expect. As we have arranged it. So you may see me before you see my letter, dearest Carry.

But for now I remain,
Eternally yours,
Patricia June Gluckendown

Dear Caroline,
The expected knock came at my door this morning. Only it wasn't Steven. It was Gary, wielding the private letter I had written you about my dream. Two other men were with him. They said they were worried about me, and forcibly charged their way into my front living room. I asked if they were here to escort me to the circus. I think one of them may have been the Eye. One of them said, 'Yes, we are here to take you to the circus. Can you tell us why we're going there?' I said, 'Certainly. We're off to find Gary's wife Caro and bring her back to live among decent friends and neighbours.'

They asked who 'we' was. I said, 'Steven and I, of course. Though you are all most welcome to come along. We're taking the bus for the first part of the journey. We've only booked for two, but I am sure we could squeeze on a couple of extras.'

They asked very nicely if they could drive me to the circus themselves. I said, 'Oh well, but it's an awfully long way. And besides, we ought to wait for Steven.'

They quizzed me a little about Steven, so I relayed the circumstances of our meeting. They asked if I had his phone number. I admitted, a little indignantly, that I did not. That it wasn't necessary. Steven knew where to find me. He should be here at any moment. The clock tower was chiming the half hour. So I made a nice cuppa and we sat down to wait for Steven. And we waited. And we waited. The clock tower was chiming the hour. Gary asked if I wouldn't come for a nice drive out into the country, to try and find the circus out there. He promised that there would be ice creams on the way, so I reluctantly agreed. After all, you might have been in my own back yard this whole time, Caroline. I told Gary off for snooping at my private letters to you. It turned out he'd only seen the one description of my dream.

We all piled into the car, and drove out the west way, past the cliffs and around to the harbour. It was a lovely night, with the sun setting the sky on fire in a haze of dusky pink, ringing bronze. We eventually arrived at a small little community nestled on the banks of a river. I was ushered into one of the offshooting houses, and shown a small room. Gary said he would visit me often. I asked him to bring Bertie on his next visit, for he must be missing me dreadfully. He promised me that he would take care of my fish, and arrange for a new volunteer to take over my Meals On Wheels position at City Central. I asked if Steven could be traced and also brought to visit, preferably wearing his raven's suit. Gary said he would see what he could do.

Gary says he will continue the search for you until I am safely back at home. My apologies, dear Caroline, but I cannot come in search of you just at this moment. I shall write again tomorrow.

Patricia

Caro,
I have been talking to a little bald man. He took me into a tiny office and explained the circumstances of detainment. I said I thought I was on holiday. He said, 'Oh yes, right you are.' He asked me a lot of silly questions about you, and then about Bertie.

I mentioned that you were with the circus, but that I bore you no grudges and would soon be coming to find you and bring you home. He asked me to list a lot of words connected with water. He asked me about my mother. I waited, trying to think of something interesting to say. He looked at the clock on his wall, then shuffled nervously through some papers in his desk drawer. I thought a bit more, but very slowly.

'The most vacuous of spaces can be the most confining,' I murmured softly to myself.

'What?' He jerked suddenly upright.

'Nothing.' I twiddled a loose strand of hair. 'She's coming back', I said, 'from the circus. She'll be home soon.'

'Patricia. There are one hundred people in a room. Ninety-nine of them think the monkey is black and one of them thinks the monkey is red. Who do we believe?'

'The monkey.'

'Now you're just being difficult.'

'Am not.'

Poor little bald man. He looked so bored. Pause. Sigh. Glance at clock. Spin on chair. Stare at self in mirror. Spin on chair. Stare at left shoulder. Switch field of vision to right breast. Look quickly away at cobweb in corner of ceiling.

'Caroline Fields is on a management course in Australia.'

'Says who?'

'Says her husband, Gary.'

Under breath, 'Lying fiend. Bloody Judas.'

'I beg your pardon?'

'Nothing.'

Pause. Sigh. Glance at clock. Spin on chair. Stare at self in mirror. Spin on chair. Stare at right shoulder. Reach into desk drawer. Bring out pill packet. Hand over tablets.

'I would like you to start taking these, Patricia, until you are well.'

'I'm perfectly all right. It's Caro you should be after.'

'Nobody is against you. We are all on your side. We want what's best for you.'

Under breath, 'Bullshit.'

'You spoke?'

'Just a frog in the throat.'

He handed me a Vicks cough lolly. 'You are to take two every day before eating.'

'Cough lollies?'

'Please don't make this any harder than it has to be. Be a good girl for Gary, hmm?'

'I have a lover,' I said, just to get him going.

'Oh, really?'

'Yes. His name's Steven. He dresses up in a raven's suit in his spare time.'

He took out a pen. 'Ah-ha. Right. I'll just note that under personal details then, shall I? Has lover. Lover has sound sense of humour. Righto. That's that then. We'll be meeting for a little chat same time next week then, won't we?'

'Not if I can help it.'

He ushered me out the door, and I went for a stroll through the gardens. I'm frightfully bored. The other happy campers aren't all that good for social chit chat. Most of them spend their time staring at blank walls. The ones who speak to me do so in staccato sentences, fragmented speech, as though the words themselves were broken shards of mirrors they had found lodged upon their tongues. I shall have my Eye Reports forwarded to me here. That way at least I can check up on your progress. I do hope the dairy daughter will be all right without me. I guess if she gets too bored she can stare at Moray's corpse. Dinner bell!

Patty

Dear Carry,
Received the fourth Eye Report today. It must have been forwarded to my new address. Thank the Lord for the efficient postal service. That Rasputin certainly sounds like a trick! I guess I shall be seeing him soon enough. Steven also popped in today, fully outfitted. He even had a worm dangling from his beak. It was strangely orange in colour, and appeared to have watery tomato sauce dripping from the end of it. He mentioned his brother again, and we have agreed to head for the circus early next week. We shall have to go incognito, Steven in his raven outfit, and myself . . . well, I shall see what we can russle up. Must go, terribly excited.

Love P

Dear Caro,
Outfit = tick.
Transport = tick.
Steven = tick.
Map = tick.

We can only wait.

Pat

Dearest Caroline,
Tonight is the night. We are heading for the coast in Steven's car. I can hardly wait. There is a knock. I must go. I shall see you before you receive my next letter.
    Patricia

IV

Willy

There was a candle in the room. It made the curtains glow. The candle went out. Then the candle was on. Then it was black. Then the candle was glowing on the curtains. The curtains were green. Momma was in the room. Momma was yellow. Her hair was hanging down and her face was wet. The dog had its tongue upon my forehead. It felt cool and damp. The dog was howling. The dog sounded like Jim.

Go on, said Jim, go on and blow them out. Red was watching. Red was holding Momma's hand. Momma's hand had the knife. The blade of the knife became yellow and then brown. Sticky. The ice in the water was cold. A cube became stuck in my throat. Jim handed me the cake. That's too much, said Red, he'll make himself sick. My chest was heaving, and the room was sliding. The floor was coming up, then going down. Jim was thumping my back.

There was a sack in the back seat. Red was moving the circle from side to side. The dog was purring beneath the metal. Clank. Shit, said Red. There was a man, giving printed paper. To Red. Sorry, said Red. And shut that fucking kid up, said the other man. Yes, said Red. Red moved the circle from side to side and moved the brown sack. Blocks fell out. Plants fell out. We came to our house. Red took the sack up to the door. He smelt of salt and sugar flowers. The car smelt of salt and sugar flowers. Somebody was howling. The dog was howling.

The kitchen light was on. It was bright. Heat was coming from the corner where Momma was. Jim was sitting on a stool with paper on his lap. His eyes moved across the paper. Say Hello, said Momma. Red put down the sack. Momma took out a plant and put it into the heat. I heard it dying. Momma put the blocks into the metal. Jim! Say Hello, said Momma. Hello Willy, said Jim. Have you had a nice day? No, I said. Jim said, Why Willy, what's happened now? I said, The plant's dying, then Jim began to choke. Then the dog began to choke. Momma gave him some water. Then they all began to choke and I did too.

I was choking. There was a cloth in my mouth. The cloth was red. The tongue of the dog was red. The dog was howling. It was sitting on top of the box. The box was open.

Jim was looking inside the box. Jim was cold. Jim was still. There was water on his face. There was a plant in the box, with hands and feet and a head with hair.

The hair had a colour. It was brown, like Jim and me.

Two cups brown, said Momma, and two cups white. That way everybody's happy. You kids are getting enough fibre, and Red's not clucking on about birdseed. And honey to make it sweet for you, Willy. The heat was bubbling. Momma had killed the plant. Red came into the kitchen. Damn that boy, he said. When's he gonna get some sense. The house was being hit by a hammer. Momma went to talk to the hammer. Momma came back with Diana. Spends every bloody cent at the pub, said Red. We went out of the house together. I stared at the hammer which clung on to the house. We moved through the space in the hedge. The edges of the red flowers were curling around their centres. They hung on to the green. Drops of blood were on the ground. They came from Diana's yellow fingers.

Momma was yellow. Her hand was on my head. It felt cold. My head was on fire. The candle was on then off then on then off and Momma's hand went on and off with the candle. The dog was throwing itself against the door. The siren was ringing in the kitchen from where it sat next to the metal. It sat on a plank. It was black. There was a man next to Momma. The dog's cloth tongue was on my face.

The man was pulling on my legs. The dog was stuck in the room next door. The dog was kicking its legs against the wall. It beat like a drum.

The gate is behind us. Diana and I walk along the grey wood. The grey wood has squares on it. The squares are white. When I bend down I can rub them off with my finger. The seagulls are white. They are yelling at me. I run away from Diana and from the seagulls. They follow me on their strings. I have seen them under the sheet in the park. Diana chases me. I start to choke. Diana chokes too. She catches my hand. Diana says, 'You're a box of birds today', and we both choke. We are choking. We have left Momma with the two browns and the two whites. We have left Red with the circle, counting paper. We walk faster than the seagulls. Two girls go past holding hands. Their eyes are on my face. I put my face out for them. They start to choke. Diana pulls me harder. I make a noise like a seagull. One of the girls has brown hair. Jim has brown hair. Jim does not walk. Jim puts his head into the paper fire. The paper fire makes his hair go brown. The girl with brown hair is carrying a paper fire. I run after her to get the paper fire for Jim. It is green. It has white marks on, like the grey wood. This will make Jim's eyes flame.

'Shit, look out,' says the white hair girl.

'What's he want, what's he want¿' says the brown hair girl.

'He's after that chemistry textbook,' says the white hair girl.

'Let him have it,' says the brown hair girl.

I am running with the paper fire. Diana is chasing me. She is not choking, but I am. Diana reaches out for the paper fire. I make a sound like the seagull. Then I make a noise like the dog. Diana's face is yellow. She has brown hair like Jim and the girl. She is cold like the metal. I stop. Her eyes look at my face. My shoes are red like the blood flowers. I look at the paper fire. Jim is reading the paper fire. His face is flame. He is eating Momma's two brown and two white dead plants. He is short. He has on a red suit and a red nose. He has a hoop around his head.

He hands me a red circle on a stick. I hand the fire to Diana. The white hair girl takes it. The brown hair girl has her eyes on my face.

'What the fuck's wrong with him?' she says.

'Hasn't your mother taught you it's rude to stare?' says Diana.

'Just askin',' says the brown hair girl, and takes her book from the white hair girl.

The brown hair girl moves her cloth over the fire. She holds the fire at the end of her hand. Then the dog starts to make a noise and he won't stop because he has seen his tongue on the fire and on the line and he howls like the seagulls under the cloth at the park and Diana says Oh Christ and she drags me and the girls are white and brown and brown and white and the dog is brown like Jim when he is on fire next to the plank.

The fire was coming up from the four white cups and heat. The fire was on tiny sticks. Momma's face was yellow with it. There were curtains of hard water on the outside of the window.

'Blow out the candles, Willy!'

'Fifteen!' said Red. 'Don't time fly.'

'Eight years since . . . ' said Momma.

'Don't.' said Red. 'Just say it's seven years since we two met.'

I started to choke.

'What's he chortling about?' said Red.

I was looking at the metal ticker. It said four white cups o'clock. I made a noise like the dog outside the metal.

'Go on, give him a slice!' said Jim. 'We're all as hungry as hell.'

The blade of the knife became yellow and then brown. The yellow and brown came towards me. I put the four white cups and heat into my mouth like the dog.

'Willy!' said Momma. 'And to think of the hours that sponge took me.'

'Supermarket's just as good,' said Jim.

'Oh, go on,' said Momma, and her mouth curled up like the edges of the flowers.

The yellow and brown went down my pipe and wouldn't move. The room began to slide. I was cold. Ice was inside the metal. The metal was inside me. Jim was thumping on my back. The dog was inside the metal. The dog was sliding across the ice.

'Medicine,' yelled Momma.

Jim was running. The dog was running next to Jim. The dog was chasing a seagull. The dog was on a string. The cloth was on a string. The dog was snapping at the cloth. The cloth was pouring down my pipe. Jim was the dog was the cloth was pouring down my pipe. The dog had the end of the string in its mouth. It was pulling. The string came out and I was still.

Jim was still beside the box. The white flowers were below the head. They had water on them. They smelt of salt and sugar.

The day smelt of salt and sugar. We were on the lane that led to the park. We walked past the lake. Throw the bread to the duckies, said Diana. A big fat duck got all the bread. The lake was still. The duck was sitting on the glass. We went past the lake. We came to the hedge. Through a hole in the hedge I could see the swings. We went through the metal. The grass was dead and brown in the middle of the park.

Inside the cake was a plastic egg. Inside the plastic egg was a piece of paper with a number on it. One, two, three, four. Four numbers.

'Who's going to take him?' said Red.

'Me,' said Jim.

'I don't think he should go after this latest turn,' said Momma.

'Sure he can. He wouldn't want to miss it for the world,' said Jim.

'You take his medicine then. And make sure he doesn't get too excited. You'll set him off. And don't go near the trains. Take him straight to the park and bring him straight home. Don't allow him to be abducted by any clowns.'

'Yes, yes, yes.'

We went through the gap. I was cold. Everything was white. Nothing red was hanging on to nothing green. Nothing grey was on the ground. Somebody had made a man. He had an orange nose. There was a word on the snow. I couldn't know what it meant. I couldn't understand any words. Then there were no words there, only the snow. I was wearing my boots. Jim had on a brown scarf. Our feet left holes, where the shadows fell in. We ran to beat our shadows.

The lane led to the park. There were no ducks. The glass was frozen over.

Somebody had drawn with a pen right across the glass. Children were strapping their white pens on to their feet. The marks on the glass were black and hollow. They were like the marks on the cake before the blade. We were still running in case we fell down next to our feet. The park was not there. There was a big cloth in its place. The big cloth was green. There was a black hole in the big cloth. Jim gave the paper to a man. We moved through the black hole and into the big cloth. Nothing outside was in the big cloth. There were lines in the big cloth. The seagulls walked along the lines. A man with a tomato on his nose was sitting on top of a circle and a line. Jim went away and I was left. I stared at all the faces. They moved at the same time. All the mouths opened and all the eyes shut at the same time. I looked up. Holes of light filtered through the cloth. Jim came back with a flower on a stick. Inside was a dead tree. I ate it. It changed colours like the garden.

The grass had changed from green to brown. On the far side of the park past the brown grass were the swings. The red one was the best. A boy had elastic inside his mouth. Pop, it said.

The hair was brown. Jimmy was looking at the hair on the plant. Water was everywhere. The dog was howling. White flowers were everywhere. They had red hearts and bled like the dog. The dog was bleeding. The dog was chasing a bird.

A dog was with the boy. The dog ran ahead to the swings. I ran faster than the dog and faster than my shadow. Our shadows fell where our feet were. The dog was white and brown. I was at the swings. Pop, said the elastic. Diana was looking at her arm. It sat on the end of her arm. It made a noise like the swing. Back and forward. It slowed down. It slowed. I wanted it to stop. Pop, said the elastic. I wanted Diana to stop looking. I knew what it would say. Four white o'clock. It always said four white o'clock. I got on the swing next to the boy. I made it go to make Diana stop. Back and forward. It slowed down. I slowed down. The boy stopped his swing. It kept going. I couldn't stop it and the dog came nearer with the green and red garden in its mouth and the dog was chasing the boy and it kept going and the red came closer and the red came around me and I then the dog was all that was red and the boy was chasing and the dog was chasing and the bird and then red and green and the dog was howling and it stopped.

It stopped with a brown plant. Jim held my hand to keep away the faces. The faces opened their mouths. We walked across the people. The man with the tomato walked away. A big brown dog came into the cloth. It came through a black hole on the other side of the cloth. The dog had a rope around its neck. A man was holding the rope. The big brown dog was quiet. The man and the dog left the cloth through the black hole. A girl with white hair came in past the dog.

She walked into a box. She fell in half.

Everything fell in half. The dog and the bird became two dogs and two birds and they came in close. Then everything was backing away.

The faces were backing away.

'So, Willy, how does it feel to be an old man? Look,' said Jim. 'Here he comes.'

A man walked into the tent. He held a dead plant in his hand. The dead plant shot up into the ceiling. The man climbed the ceiling. The man walked across the ceiling, across the line. The faces were closing on sticks on green on red. The man was running. The man was running out of the ceiling. Jim was looking at his four white wrists.

'No, it's not,' said Jim, 'but he'll be here soon. How does it feel Willy? Not long now and you'll be as old as me. You'll catch up.'

The man ran right out of the ceiling. Another man came in through the ceiling.

'Here he is!' said Jim.

Water was all over Jim's face. I stood where the wood had been. I could still see the box. I stood where the tunnel had been. I could still see Jim. I took two steps.

Two stopped. The dog swallowed the bird. I started to choke.

'Four white,' I said, 'two brown.'

I choked and choked. The swing kept moving.

The man moved in through the ceiling and stood on the line. He dropped and swooped on his line. The faces were moving. He dropped down to the floor and ran across it to the big brown dog. The big brown dog was moving inside a circle. The circle was white on the ground. The big brown dog moved on the line. Inside a glass cage the dog swam around and around. It grew bigger. It grew too big for the cage. It broke the glass.

There was glass on the floor. There was a line from the ceiling. The plant was holding the line.

The line swung out with me on the end of it. I jumped and Diana caught me. We walked through the space on this side of the park. Everywhere was green and red and yellow. The plants were in the heat. We came out into the grey wood. The grey wood stretched away like a line. The dog was not there. We walked on the grey wood.

'When's that brother of yours going to go out and get a job, then?' said Diana, and I started to choke. 'I know he hasn't had it easy, but it's been eight years. Red's as good as a father to him now. And God knows he's been absolutely terrific with you. Not that they couldn't have managed without me, mind, but there's a lot of men out there who would have run a mile the minute they'd seen that a woman was so . . . encumbered. But, boy, once he got to know you . . . he's just been a marvel. An absolute marvel.'

We walked on through the red and yellow and green. It smelt of sugar.

Everything smelt of sugar. Momma came to the door. 'Come away, Jim,' she said. Jim stood up and took the dog away with him.

The big brown dog moved out of the cloth. We were outside. Everything was grey. The ground was melting. Our shadows melted like butter into the ground. We walked across our shadows. We started to walk.

Along the grey wood and down to the houses. We went inside the dead plant's house and Diana bought some paper fire for Jim. He wraps it around his head and sets his head on fire. We went on further. We went in through a hedge and up to a hole. A lady came.

'Jeez, Diana, long time no see,' she said.

'This is Willy,' said Diana.

'Well, hello Willy,' said the lady. 'Come on in.'

We moved in through the hole. Inside, everything was pale and washed. The walls were washed. I sat down.

'What'ya been up to, then?' said the lady.

'Just looking after this one and working part-time at the hospital,' said Diana.

'I swear, you must have the patience of a saint,' said the lady.

'What else could I do?' said Diana.

'What you mean?'

'It's all I'm qualified for.'

I moved across the floor to where the ground rose in jumps. I moved up the jumps.

'Come on. You could always go back and get into something else. You're versatile.'

'No. Anyway, tell me about yourself. You still on the dole or what?'

'Nah. Working part-time down with Greg.'

'At the garage?'

'Yeah. And keeping the accounts and stuff.'

I moved up the jumps. At the top was dark. I moved in through the darkness.

'Willy! WILLY! SHIT! Why's he move so fast?'

'He's probably mucking around in the garden. Don't panic, Di, he can't have gone too far.'

'WILLY! WILLY!'

I was inside the darkness. I moved in through another hole. I was in a room. I pulled across the wood.

'Willy!! Have you checked upstairs?' 'Yes that's where he'll be' thump thumpety thump thump up the jumps one two 'WILLY!' through the click it was white 'Willy! shit I'll kill him'

'Now calm down he'll be hiding somewhere' then out!

'Shit, Willy! You scared the living daylights out of me!'

The ground was melting and turning grey.

'She'll never know,' said Jim. 'Come on, birthday treat.'

Down the grey wood and along past the houses. We walked by the water. Specks of colour were on the water. A circle went around the water. A little boy and a big boy stood next to the water. We moved past. Everything smelt of salt. Then I couldn't see the water any more and everything started to rattle and shake and smell of smoke and the air was grey and hot and was coming from where we stood. We climbed up on to another circle and looked down at the moving noise and smoke.

'Let's see if we can spit,' said Jim, and water fell from our mouths. I didn't see it land. The noise and smoke were moving away. We moved across.

'Time to go home,' said Jim, looking at his watch.

We moved across the circle.

We moved into a circle of light. The light went out. Then I was in darkness. I lay down. I stopped there. I smelt the sugar.

Momma was in the doorway with some sugar in her hand. She put the flowers in the wood box. We moved away.

Jim took my hand and we went on along the grey wood.

V

JIM

Once inside the house, I saw that the front room was in chaos. Policemen, doctors, the whole works. But I couldn't think about Willy lying there on the floor, surrounded by officialdom. All I could think about was his fifteenth birthday. That seemed real. All the rest of this seemed artificial, and I saw it only in splits and fragments of light, as if somebody were holding shields over my eyes, then jerking them away suddenly, then putting them in place again. My mother was crying, and Red had raised himself from the sofa to put his arm around her. I didn't want to hang around, arms at my sides, useless and helpless. I went upstairs and locked the door to my room. I lay upon the floor, staring at the relief ornament which decorated the ceiling around the light bulb. I was finding it difficult to concentrate, what with all the noise rising up from down in the front room, so I threw some Bach on to the stereo, cranked up the volume and switched off my table lamp. Then I lay there in the dark, the music pounding through my temples, and thought about Willy and what things would be like if he was dead. I didn't want him to die, but we all knew that he would be lucky to live much past fifteen and he'd been going for two years. Running on borrowed time. What annoyed me the most was not the fact that he was going to die but the fact that most people thought he was stupid. Willy was just different. I moved towards the table, pulled out a drawer, got out my manuscript and felt over the top page in the dark.

The police cars were leaving. I turned down the music so I could hear Mum and Red talking. Willy was quiet. But I knew he'd be in the lounge, all right now, safe now, alive, being carried up to his bedroom. He could come to Paris with me on the proceeds of my first novel. I put my chair against the door and then I pushed my table against the chair as I heard Mother and Red climbing the stairs. I didn't want to know where he'd been, or who he'd been with or what had set him off. I only wanted to write my manuscript so that we could afford to go to Paris as soon as possible. I didn't want to go to the Big Girl's Arms tomorrow. I wanted to go to a tidy, well-lit café, where I could talk to an appreciative audience about where my book was headed.

They were hammering at the door like madmen. I yelled out, Piss off, and they did. I knew what they were thinking. They'd be thinking that I was behaving exactly as I did when we found Dad swinging from the end of a rope in the attic.

The first thing I saw when I awoke in the morning were the guards I had placed across the door. Why had I done that? Obviously I had been thinking irrationally, for the doorlock would have been enough to keep out both Red and Mother. Red had gone to work early this morning, I had heard his car backing down the driveway. Mother would be cleaning the house or baking her loaves as usual. I have always liked to rise early, as it means that I can get a good two or three hours in on one of my books before the day really begins. If I had a ladder or a pear tree or a drainpipe outside my bedroom window I might be able to climb out of the house without being caught and made to stuff down porridge and eggs. I rose from my bed and made my way to the window, which was banging in the breeze, pulling it to, drawing the curtains against the blackening sky. This is what we have learnt to do, when the weather gets stormy. I imagined her, my ice-cream angel, my dairy girl, huddled in the room with me, and then the ground fell away.

This was the first time I had felt it. The room began to spin and I began to forget everything. Everything was slipping away. Patricia Gluckendown was sitting with one leg flung casually over the window ledge, writing her letters to Caro, day in, day out. I imagined that it was night, and that was why the sky was so black. My killer hero was crouching on the wardrobe railing like a vulture about to swoop. He wanted a name. I hadn't wanted to give him one. I called him Ringer. I thought more about Ringer and the name didn't seem to match the man. No name would ever match any man.

Willy was howling next door. I was so happy that he was alive and we would soon be on a plane to Paris together.

Bash, bash, bash.

'Jim, porridge's up!'

I snapped out of my delirium and looked out at the orange sky that the shepherd had requested through mail order. The sky was ringing this morning and that was why I would call him Ringer. The wolves were howling from the snowy ledge near the ravine, and Caro sat gently stroking the white fang of one beast. I went downstairs, and the Russian bride poked her head in through the kitchen window and handed me a bowl of porridge, which I ate in desultory silence. I finished every last coagulating mouthful, then sat at the table staring at the wall and waiting for Ringer. The patterns of light on the wall shifted, and then I was playing host to his guest.

VI

Ringer

The old ticker kept turning on over, and every tick made my blood grow hotter and hotter. I thought about how the bluebells'd be coming around and looking for Pop and how they'd then be after me and Kylo'd never be the one who'd end up inside.

The road kept on moving away behind us and I felt hatred surge up inside me cold and metallic and one-sided like the blade of a knife. I imagined the blade going into the back of Kylo's neck and all the red stuff gushing out in tones of pink and black like a water-colour painting of a pretty sunset. First it would be hot, then warm, then cold. Nobody else had wanted to come in the car with us. They had wanted to watch, 'cause first they was yelling with their gobs open like they was trying to catch flies and then the flies must've flown in and they must've been gagging on them, 'cause they wasn't making no noise no more. I was thinking and everything and then I must've fallen asleep, 'cause the sun was coming up and the sky was like it was on fire or covered in Pop's blood or something, and Kylo was pissing against a brick wall on the side of the road. He hitched up his jeans and walked real slowly over to the car window.

'Where we gonna do it, then?'

'You answer me, pretty boy. You're the one who

put the spade in.'

I chomped down hard on my tongue and tightened the wire that ran from my temples down to my jaw, so as to keep from saying anything which might offend Kylo.

'I say we just keep right on driving. The last thing we want to do is to bury him near any towns, or places where folks is living. And we want to make it deep, like, so that your Pop's not floating up to the surface with the first rainfall. And we want to make it in the forest, or in the hills, yeah, so that Old Mother Nature helps us with her natural hideaway spots. You hear what I'm saying?'

I nodded my block in dumb agreement.

'Come on. Let's hear it. What you got to say for yourself then?'

I shook my block.

'Right. Let's keep it that way. Only you get in the front now. It won't go down well if it looks like I'm chauffeuring you all round the country. And this is a favour, right? So just you bear that in your little mindy-mind and we'll think about you returning the gesture when I takes you back into the town. And you set your head about thinking up a nice place where you were on the night when your father died, or you think about whether your father was kidnapped or where he's gone to, or you think about leaving the country. 'Cause only you knows just how you is going to explain to that uncle of yours just what has happened to his favourite brother all of a sudden. So either you had better go for a little overseas trip or your father has flown the country, like, and is not, right as we speak, like, sitting in twenty pieces in the boot of a Holden. Right?'

Kylo has quite a temper when he really gets fired. So I nodded and kept my block on the old tight wire.

Anyway, he was right. Somehow I'd have to leave the country or think about getting a new name or something. People do that sort of thing, from time to time. Just quit on their families and take off overseas and never come back home. Only I got no family, so I was really just as good as a free man. If you forgot, of course, about the rotting father in the boot. And the uncle waiting back at home. A couple of minor stumbling blocks, like I said. But nothing that Kylo and I couldn't think our noggins around. So I began to feel quite good, like, and all sort of secretive and glowing and like I might really have the chance for a new life somewhere else, and like it really was a great thing after all that I had put the spade into Pop or I might not have ended up with this great opportunity after all. I got around to thinking how good it would be to get away from Plymouth and all the people who had known me since I had first poked my head out of the cave and into the bright light of day. It doesn't do a bloke good to stay around in the same town all his life. It's not healthy. A fella could end up doing something he later regretted.

We buried him underneath the bridge. After we'd been driving for another four hours and been right over the top of the range, we came to a river where the bridge extended down from the hills and into the marsh all stinking and brown on the other side. There was a half-rotting cow carcass sunken down into the mud, so Kylo said that it looked as though it might make a pretty good spot to put the old bugger under, seeing as it looked like things decayed well and quickly in this marsh. I was the one that got to open the boot and take the bits of the old guy out. We'd put him into a sack, so I just lifted him out in one go and stuck him on to the ground, while Kylo stood around looking kind of sick and kind of interested at the same time. There was no one around, only the noise of a bird flying out over the swamp and the telegraph wires stretching back and back as far as the eye could see. We'd pulled over on to a grassy strip at the side of the road, sort of like the kind of place you'd come with your folks for a family picnic, so we had a wee walk down to where the cow was. Kylo was carrying the same spade that we'd done Pop in with, and I felt cold and shivery and miserable looking at it.

'Get diggin',' grunted Kylo, and I obeyed, as usual, putting Pop down on top of the old cow. Flies were hovering around pretty good now, in much the same way as the boys had been hanging around last night. To watch the action, and to see that the action wasn't anything they mightn't do themselves if it came to the crunch and they'd really got sick of somebody. If they'd really got sick of an uncle and a father constantly setting up a front, like an enemy, and doing the best to make a life resemble hell. So I set to hacking up the ground, with all those flies looking on with their four pairs of eyes apiece. And when I'd got to about six foot I started to put Pop in. He stunk pretty bad, and I was keen just to hiff the whole sack in the hole in one fell swoop, but Kylo reckoned we ought to bury him a limb at a time, sort of distribute him over the whole swamp so that he might not be recognisable. He said it was either that or knock out all his teeth and mutilate his face and hands. So I got down to it and started digging six-foot holes all over the marsh. A small cloud of flies gathered wherever I took Pop. Kylo brought me over the hacksaw we'd used to chop up Pop, and then went back to where we'd parked the car and sat on the grass puffing away on the end of a fag. I was careful to put all his parts in different locations, and even chopped off and threw a bit of cow into a few of the grave sites, in case he ever got found and somebody would have a fun old time of it, trying to work out if he was a minotaur or what.

I took off my shirt, even though there was still frost and spikes of ice around on the marsh, and began to plan my life. I thought I might go back home with a beard and maybe, like, somebody else's hair and a pair of dark shades, and steal Pop's chequebook and ID from the top drawer next to his bed and take off for the States. 'Course I'd have to travel under his passport, but that'd solve problems with people figuring out where Pop'd got to all of a sudden. The boys would shut their gobs about it. They'd miss me, but it would be good for them, especially for Kylo, who never did appreciate all the shit I took on his behalf. Doing his dirty work, and distracting the bluebells while he put the gun in at stores or put the plank over on some old geezer. I'd just put Pop under, stop in at some small town on the way home to get a bit of a 'guise on, sneak into home, grab the passport and the rest of the guff, race to the bank, then head on out to the airport. If Kylo didn't want to agree with me, well, he didn't have to. I'd hand in my resignation, and he'd find a replacement easy as that.

I had Pop by the hair and was about to send him happily into the ninth grave when I heard the engine start. Kylo was waving out the window and revving the engine as he backed away. I saw him toss his cigarette on the grass. The back of the Holden pulled out to the road and sped up on to and across the bridge. Son of a bitch! I'd have that fucker in the same way as I'd had Pop! We must be at least seven hundred kilometres from home. I hadn't been watching the clock, but we'd gone right through the night, and I reckoned at it being about nine now. If that bastard pimped on me! Bile was rising up in my throat like a cancer. The hatred I'd known for my father seemed a tiny pinprick compared to this vast ocean of pure steel hatred I felt for Kylo. Death by spade'd be too good for that arsehole. I'd tear him limb from limb with my bare hands in front of his own mother, then throw his still screaming head into a fiery furnace. I'd condemn him to hell for all eternity, make him re-live his death and re-live his death and re-live his death like a movie stuck on to a loop tape.

I buried my father's forearms, put my shirt back on, then staggered on to the road, still clutching the brown muddy spade and the bloody hacksaw. Fuck it all. Not even a place to chuck the weapons. I dug a hole in the grass at the side of the road and buried the hacksaw, then swung the spade over my shoulder and began walking away from the bridge.

The sun was in the middle of the sky and I was creating no shadow when I came to the first stark skeletons of trees. I walked in among the sticks for five hundred yards, dug into the ground, threw the spade into the earth and pushed dirt over with my foot. I broke boughs from the forest and covered the area with leaves and sticks. Turning around to face the road, I walked back to where I had been. The road stretched away into the distance, becoming the black point of a pencil, a full stop.

She was hollering from the porch.

'Momma, Momma, there's a man out here to see you, and he's looking kind of dirty.'

The old woman hobbled out on to the porch, dragging her right leg slowly behind her left one. Her apron was covered in smears and stains, and her veins stood out against her face as if they had been inflated by air.

'What you want?' she snarled, and I felt as if the odour of her might be enough to knock an unprepared animal out cold. I noticed she was missing both her canine teeth.

'A room for the night,' I said, real cool and casual, like I wasn't in no trouble or nothing and I might just have run into this town not at all desperate and run-down but just as a number shown on a casual toss of a die. Like I might have ended up in any town if I chose to stop there, and this one was nothing special and this room really meant nothing to me.

The woman blended perfectly with her surroundings, brown, stained, crumpled. Planks were missing from both the porch and the house itself, and the wind whistled through the gaps.

'Fer the night?' she drawled real slow, and I could tell she was playing me like a fish on a nylon line. The girl was tugging on the edges of her skirt and sucking on something that looked like chewed old kewpie doll. She was smiling to herself as she looked up at her Momma, and I couldn't help thinking that mother and daughter were in cahoots, that they'd planned for somebody like me to wander along.

'What you got all messin' up your shirt, Mista?'

'Shh, Missy! These rooms is thirty dollars a night, no meals provided. You like to sleep?'

'No,' I said, 'not much.'

'Good. 'Cause we got people coming and going through these doors all hours of the day and night, so we don't get much shut-eye. If you want a good night's rest, you'll have to go out in the garden.' She laughed. 'How far you walked tonight?'

'Not far,' I said, moving my toe so as to escape the small pool of blood that a popped blister had caused.

'You gonna stand there all night looking tired?'

'No.'

She peeled back the door and I stood gazing down a long corridor. I crossed the porch and entered. The place was decked out in plush shades of maroon, and each door had a number on it.

'Common room's in the dead centre of the place. This here's your night room, where you can take your rest, though I don't guarantee you'll get much of that.'

She drew a key from the large hoop she had around her belt, and unlocked the door. A hazy beam of light fell from the window on to the floor, and in the ray I saw small motes of dust floating and blowing on the breeze. A Gideon's Bible sat on a dresser next to the bed, which was covered in a thin white candlewick bedspread. A small bunch of dried lavender sat on the windowsill, next to a potted geranium and a pocket mirror. A table and a chair sat in the middle of the room, the chair pulled out at an angle to invite sitting.

'Nothing much happens here,' she said, 'not during the day. During the day we just wait for the night. But we don't wait in here. Come on, I'll show you.'

I nodded, and we proceeded back out into the hallway, with the girl still hanging on behind her mother. We passed five or six rooms and turned to the left once, then left again. The hag unlocked another door, and we entered a room painted a light pastel shade of green.

'This here's the common room I told you about. The girls are all here now, 'cause things ain't been that busy tonight.'

Women hung draped from sofas and chaises-longues, some absentmindedly painting toenails, others plaiting hair or applying make-up. Many of them were playing cards, scrabble, snakes and ladders. They wore lace, velvet, satin, organza, in shades of blue, red, green. Insatiability hung in the air like the scent of a long-forgotten perfume. Gilt-framed paintings hung on the walls, and I could barely make out the Christian names printed beneath them. Joan, Simone, Oliver, Emma,

Henri, Charles, Gus. A bird in a wicker cage chirped a cacophonous note. I excused myself from this scene, from this dreadful rag-and-bone shop of femininity, to go to the bathroom. 'Down the hall and to your left.' As I exited, I noticed one of the girls following behind me. I trod softly on the carpet. Her footsteps fell slightly out of time with my own. I turned left as instructed, not daring to turn around. Was she a spy? Was she concealing a weapon on her person? Rifle, baton, knife? I walked a little faster, though not so much as to excite her. She quickened her pace. My heart beat like the organ of a lunatic in my chest. Up ahead, I could see the door marked 'Toilets'. I put my hand on the fingerprinted steel panel. Her hand pressed down upon mine. Still I feared to turn around. I pushed the door open and entered a cubicle. The door of the slot next to mine drew shut with a bang.

I relieved myself with a sigh, and admired the graffiti.

'What's your name?' I heard in a hushed whisper through the wall.

'What?'

'What's your name?'

'Ringer.'

'That's very pretty.'

'Thank you.'

'My name now is Sophia. We have all changed our names. We had to. She made us. Don't tell on me. Are you staying long?'

'I'm looking for work.'

'Are you on the run from the law?'

I crossed my fingers. 'No. Will she have work for me?'

She burst into laughter. 'For a man? Not unless it's making the beds during the day.'

'I'll do anything.'

'You can get that tone of desperation out of your voice for a start. The minute the matron senses that, she'll have you here for years. What room's she given you?'

'Twenty-three.'

'That's all right then.'

Footsteps came down the hall towards us. We flushed simultaneously, then walked together to the common room, passing 'the matron' who walked with the girl still clinging to her apron. I didn't see why she wore an apron, really, because she didn't look as though she would cook, herself. She looked as if she would have a servant for everything. Sophia and I retired into the common room. I felt the eyes of the women on me like hawks.

'What's he then, if not a customer?'

'Is he a freak? What's all that blood on his shirt then? Or is that tomato sauce?'

Titters of laughter.

'What room you in? What room you in?'

'You got enough space in there, not too cramped for you?'

'Hope you got you a good watch, son.'

'Here, have mine.'

Laughter. A watch flew across the room and landed in my lap. Half-past two.

'Morning or night, pretty boy?'

'We're here for you morning and night.'

'Twenty-four-hour service, sir.'

'On call, that's what we are. All you got to do is pick up your phone and dial the number.'

'Just like dialling a prayer, really, ain't it girls?'

'We're an SOS service. Send-a-slut. That's us.'

I glanced nervously at the portrait of Charles.

'What you waiting for? You want a screw? Take your pick?'

'Choose at your leisure, baby.'

'Or your own risk.'

I turned my pockets inside out and gave a nervous sideways shuffle.

'I haven't even got money for a room, let alone . . . extra services.'

'Extra services! Whoo, ain't the man got the flashest lingo then?'

'How you going to pay for your room then, lovely? You gonna hire yourself out as well?'

'I thought I might offer to make beds and do dishes.'

'Well! We don't need that! We's already got ourselves a charlady.'

The matron entered, humming 'Jingle Bells' softly under her breath and jangling her keys in time.

'We'll find some way for you to pay for your room, huh?'

'Sure, we'll find a way. He's got orifices, ain't he?'

I felt myself breaking into a cold nervous sweat, and imagined that I heard Pop laughing from somewhere beyond the grave.

The matron turned to a girl who sat buffing her toenails. 'Customer for you, Fay. He's waiting upstairs. Room 177.' She took another key from her belt and threw it towards the girl, then gave me a penetrating glare. 'You didn't mention that you didn't have no money on ya. You know you should have told me that. That's withholding information, that is. We could have you for that.'

'I'll leave.'

Laughter echoed around the four walls.

'Where you gonna go? There ain't nowhere for miles, least not this side of the border.'

'What border?'

'The border you just crossed, darling. Where you buried your Poppa.'

'What?'

'We heard what you done. Customer drove overhead when you were under there doing all that digging. Came straight here and reported to us. Said he seen you burying a man, and that same man been reported missing in a town, and the son missing too, and that son sound just like you look.'

Sniggers and muffled grunts of disapproval.

'I think you must be mistaken.'

'We could hide you here and hire you out. You'll be all right. Big Thomas likes his boys petite, doesn't he, girls?'

Then I was running right and turning right and running right again, and past the rooms and down the corridor and right out on to the road and cursing Kylo at the top of my lungs and wishing to God that it had been me and not my father dead and buried and under that bridge with the traffic zooming back and forth day and night and day and night.

Out on the road, all the shops were shut down. The town had the stale air of a public holiday, as if it had seen no change of weather and no movement since the last winter. I raced the bouncing tussock down the main street, passing stores, a gas station and run-down houses. I ran until the houses turned into grass and the grass turned into shrub and the shrub turned into forest, and then turning around I saw the gas station and all the stores and all the houses melting into the dust. I felt a cold hand on my shoulder, and turned around to see the face of my uncle bearing down upon me.

'You're in an awful hurry. And there's no need. Very soon you're going to have all the time in the world.'

VII

KATE

God I hate ice-cream. I hate every last little flavour. I hate hokey-pokey and vanilla and chocolate and goody-goody gum-drops and strawberry and boysenberry ripple. All day, all fucking day I hand them across the counter and take the money: eighty cents for a kiddy cone, a dollar twenty for a single scoop, a dollar eighty for a double scoop, and twenty cents extra if you want the whole thing chocolate dipped. I've learnt to switch off. I've learnt to put myself somewhere else. And today I was thinking, as I handed another caramel fudge across the counter, isn't it funny how you remember things in flashes?

My memory functions like a strobe light. Full glare, flicker, half light, flicker, flicker, blackout. What I remember now is that as a kid I had a mate called Maria, and what I remember about Maria is that she had that sort of ginger hair that makes you think of girls who rode horses in novels about boarding schools. And to match the hair she had that light, pasty, translucent skin that reminds you of blue-veined cheese. The rest of us kids used to give her shit about that hair; well, you know what kids are like. Little shits that we were. I used to deal her out with the best of them, but eventually I must've felt sorry for her or something, because we were friends by the time I was nine. It was like that at our school; they'd take the shit out of you for about six months, and then you'd be all right. It was sort of an initiation ritual, a way of sorting out what you could stand and what you couldn't. It was a case of steeling yourself in order to gain a bit of respect. I'd learnt to do that when I arrived at the school, and I watched Maria do it too when she first arrived, and she never cried once, not even when about twenty of us ganged up and pelted her with gravel, and so I made friends with her. If they'd pelted me with gravel I'd have pimped to the headmaster, but Maria just stood there and took it, and after that I knew she'd make a great mate.

We used to stand together in assembly and sing the school song, tacky as all hell, and on Anzac Day the whole school would chant along after the headmaster. *In the morning, and at the going down of the sun, we will remember them.* I'm not sure we knew who we were commemorating. Anzac Day was something to do with dead people and wars in other countries that we were somehow involved in and Flanders Field and paper poppies being sold on the street. I don't think we were too interested in that stuff, but we liked the chant. Anzac Day as a whole had overtones of old men with gammy legs and war wounds. Also, men who had been to war could get bits of shrapnel embedded in them, which meant that stray bits of bullets and bomb had got in under the surface and couldn't be got out again. Maria's grandfather had fought, but my only living grandfather had been a conscientious objector which was less exciting. It meant that he couldn't get work after the war was over, and had been harassed while drinking at the pub. To die in service for your country was something romantic and amazing. To refuse to go to war meant nothing but shame. These were the stories we were told. This was the fiction.

The war was only ever a fiction, something which had captured the imaginations of our teachers. We had been born so long after the event that not even our relatives talked of it. It was something that had happened in the past and only the romanticism had filtered down to us. The trenches and the uniforms, the dead buried in foreign countries. The colour red. The war was not even a memory or the dream of a memory; it was an action adventure story, something made up for adult entertainment and thought about only by boys when they played with plastic men. And by Maria and me on Anzac Day.

We were in the last year of primary school the year we made friends, and our parents were just beginning to let us go out at night, for an hour or two, as long as we were home before eight. People do different things to escape to somewhere else: they read books or they watch TV or they listen to the radio or they go to the carnival. At this stage I was spending a lot of my spare time down in the cellar, scraping plaster off the walls and listening to the sounds of Mum and Dad yelling at each other and smashing plates and glasses. Fucking awful. Shit. Foul language. Mum and Dad hate me to talk like that; say it means I'm cheap. They used to say they'd wash my mouth out with soap, but they've stopped that now.

They're quite ashamed of me in some ways, my Mum and Dad. Not that they believe in class levels or anything, but if they did, they'd say that I should raise myself up a rung or two on the ladder. Dad has this chicken theory which (as far as I can work it out) entails 'climbing up the perch' so that you might 'shit on anyone underneath you' before they 'shit on you'. I think this is related to 'Life's a shit sandwich: the more bread you got, the less shit you eat.' This one confuses me. We sell a lot of bread at the dairy, but we still have to do the shitty work, like cleaning the floor.

I quite like my job. Just because I haven't done like Damon's done, and gone to work in Dad's company in the junior management section; just because I *choose* to work in a dairy, they think I'm stupid. Anyway, only one of us has to work at Dad's company. I mean, when Dad gets sick and refuses to leave the house, Damon can just take over for the week, or the month, or however long it takes Dad to become well again. No fuss, and it's all nice and easy, and no one knows anything about it. They just think Dad's taken the time off to go trout fishing or something.

I think that they had high hopes for me once, Mum and Dad. I was always good at French. Mum tried to push for me to go to teachers' college, but I didn't know any Maori and I couldn't play the piano so they wouldn't let me in. Anyway, I'm happy where I am. I like working near the sea; there are advantages to that. If you poke your head round the front door of the shop, you can see the ocean and hear those white birds screaming like lunatics. People take their dogs down to crap on the sand, and when the tide goes out all kinds of driftwood and kelp and sea tulips wash up on to the beach. Also some scrap metal and bits of car tyre. It's not such a clean area I work in, it's not exactly the North Shore. But it's great for collecting, that beach. I wouldn't mind getting old by this sea, better than what Damon's doing, stuck away in that office, rotting behind his laptop. After work I like to walk down by the ocean amongst the hypodermic needles and ripped condoms and the used car parts. I like the fact that it's kind of scungy down there, 'cause that reminds me of what it used to be like at the carnival, with bits of old hotdog stuck to the sides of the hall of mirrors, and candy floss melted on to the seat of the ghost train. It's nice to think about it like that. It's nice to think that other people have been there before you. Either on the beach, screwing around and shooting up, or at the carnival, screaming in mock terror so they can snuggle closer to one another.

Sometimes I think I remember the scunge of a place better than the actual place itself. But that's just the way I am. I remember in scunge, and I remember in strobe-light flickers.

The carnival is one of those things that flickers; that's why I brought it up. I remember the carnival in staccato, whereas there are other things I remember perfectly, like singing about the war, and others that my mind has erased for me. It's not that anything horrible ever happened at the carnival, it's not one of those repressed memories or whatever you call them. It's just that some days you might think about the carnival rides, and some days you might not. Depends on your state of mind, really, doesn't it? There's not room in a mind to think about everything all at once. I'm only mentioning the carnival because the other day, as I was scooping out some hokey-pokey ice-cream into a waffle cone, I suddenly got this flash of a white face, this white face behind a mask, and I couldn't quite place it. This ice-cream illusion made me give a bit of a scream, and my boss came running and I had to clean up the hokey-pokey 'cause I'd dropped it on the floor right where I stood, and I had to make the young woman a new one so that she'd go away satisfied. The customer always comes first. Then I had to have a bit of a sit-down. After all, it's not every day a plaster face comes dancing out of the hokey-pokey. All that day I kept trying to figure out where I'd seen that face, and then I remembered that it was at the carnival, with Maria, when I was fifteen, just before our friendship ended and we stopped going there. Isn't that strange? All that day I thought about that face, but when I went home I forgot all about it.

That night I dreamed that the face was attached to a body like a scarecrow's, a body made of sticks and twigs and bits of old bramble bushes. The white mask sat on top of the straw body, the nose like the beak of a bleached vulture. And I woke up sweating.

VIII

JIM

It was summer, but the time of day meant that the blue sky had a very black look. It was not raining. It hadn't rained for weeks. The desk and the chair were rattling as if a hurricane were shaking the whole house. The chair jiggled impatiently on one leg.

'Jim! Jim! Come out of there! Come down and get some breakfast! Your mother and I need to talk to you.'

Pause. Lie on floor, very still, listening only to the sound of breathing.

'Jimmy, this is important. You can't just block this out. It won't go away.'

In two, three, four, and out two, three, four.

The Russian bride was sipping vodka from a clear crystal glass, as Patricia Gluckendown poured Vitagrow into the goldfish bowl. I glared at her.

'Where the hell have you been? We've been dead worried about you.'

She smiled enigmatically.

'Jim!'

Bash, bash, bash. In two, three, four, and out two, three, four.

'Are you coming out, or are we going to have to force this door?'

'Coming!'

I pulled back the guards from the door. Red stood

panting and flushed in the hallway.

'Son . . . '

'I'm not your son.'

'Jim . . . your mother and I want to talk with you about what's happened. Right now you're probably still locked deep within the grieving process. But we've all known that this was coming for a long time. Mortality is a fact we have to learn to accept. We want you to come downstairs and talk with us.'

'What about?'

'Whatever you're feeling at the moment.'

I knew Red was pretty cut up about the whole death thing, so decided to humour him.

'Have you got my porridge ready?'

'And waiting, son.'

I headed down the stairs behind him, holding on to the wooden banister, fighting a strange vertiginous sensation.

Mother had her head on the table, and looked up red-eyed when she heard us entering the kitchen. She rushed across to embrace me, and I became encased in a rustling of starched black cotton. I kept my arms stiff down at my sides, like a mummy or an army cadet.

'Oh Jim. Don't let this crush you!'

'No, Mother.'

I moved uncomfortably backwards, and she loosened her vice-like grip. I took two steps sideways and knocked an uncooked egg from the kitchen table on to the floor, where it lay splattered like a wet sheet thrown from an upstairs laundry room.

'You're such a good boy. You were always so good with him. You had such patience. We are fully aware of the fact that none of this will be easy for you to deal with – the Lord knows, it won't be easy on any of us – and we realise that material possessions can't compensate for spiritual loss, but just to show you that we really do feel for you, and *understand* what you are going through, your father and I have bought you a small token.'

I watched a fly touch down on the clotted surface of my grey porridge which sat cooling in a blue crockery bowl. Mother nudged Red, who searched in a pocket below his stomach and produced a small parcel wrapped in red crinkling paper.

'Go on. Open it.'

I tentatively peeled back the shiny red paper, which offered up its sparkling silver insides to me. A small maroon velvet box lay in my palm.

The fly rubbed its forelegs together and walked across the surface of my breakfast.

'We know this can never make up for the loss you . . . we all . . . have suffered. But we hope it might provide a minor consolation in this hour of grief.'

Red belched and Mother shot him a filthy look. Under the twin pairs of interrogating eyes I pried open the box. It fell back on its own hinge. Mother inhaled sharply, as sharply as Red exhaled.

My first watch.

I turned it belly-up and read the brand. 'Mr Tick-Tock. Manufactured in Taiwan.'

Only the best for the sole surviving son.

'Thanks very much.' I gave them both an awkward hug.

'Now you go on and sit down and eat your porridge like a good boy.'

I sat.

'You'll need all your strength for tomorrow afternoon. There's no need for you to go out searching for a job today; you just stay at home and keep warm. Red might take you for a drive in the country.' She nudged Red.

'Where would you like to go, son?'

'To the Big Girl's Arms,' I said through a mouthful of milk, sugar and oats.

'Where?'

'He means the pub.'

'Don't you think this should be a time for the family to pull itself together, boyo?'

'Let him be, Red. You and I'll go for a nice trip to the seashore ourselves. Ice creams and a walk along the beach watching the gulls, eh?'

The beach. In my mind's eye I saw her there, handing soft chewy caramels across to the children who came in crying for sweets, pushing ten cents across the counter, bustling brown leather school satchels against one another, then she'd gaze wistfully in front of her, perhaps make herself a cone, slowly lick the drips that fell.

A wolf was scratching at the kitchen door, so I pushed back my seat and rose to let him into the warmth. He settled comfortably down by the fire and began to scratch around his muzzle, giving a few discontented howls before finally settling down with his head rested upon his forepaws.

'Time enough for mourning tomorrow avo. I think it best if each member of this family does whatever they may to come to terms with his or her own personal grief.'

I looked up, spoon poised half-way between mouth and bowl.

'Grief?' I hadn't known Red was suffering.

He belched amicably. 'If that means a few pints with the lads, then you just go on ahead down to the Arms.'

'I intend to go to Melbourne shortly.'

'Oh Jimmy, no. Don't start this nonsense again.'

'Your mother and I have told you before. You'll continue looking for a job here, and if you wish to further your academic studies overseas, then you'll be on your own with no funding from us.'

The Russian bride entered the kitchen and strapped a collar and leash on to the wolf, who then stood pawing anxiously at the collar. I said nothing, only sat staring at the wolf.

'At any rate, we know from our previous experiences of dealing with grief and other . . . nervous maladies that one must beware of inertia. Why don't you get on the phone to those mates of yours and arrange for a trip to the park out on the edge of town before going out boozing? We don't want you hanging around in your room all day. You'll work yourself into a right royal state. I think it might be best if you come for a drive with us, or go out with your friends. Keep yourself occupied. The Devil finds work for empty hands.'

'Do you have to be so didactic towards him at a time like this?'

'I'm not being didactic, love, I'm just making suggestions from the authoritative position of adulthood.'

'He needs love, not lessons.'

'I'm not trying to give him a bloody lesson. I'm trying to help.'

'You don't know what his brother meant to him!'

'Look, love, let's not fight. Emotions are running high at a time like this, and there's bound to be a whole heap of memories floating up . . . '

'Do you have to bring that up?'

'Bring what up? Would you stop trying to mollycoddle the boy! We've got to talk about the past, for chrissakes!'

'I'll start talking about the past when I want to, not when you demand it. Christ, it's always demand, demand, demand.'

'You're over-reacting.'

'*I'm* over-reacting? You're the one who started this whole thing about the past; I was just trying to protect my son from two family deaths!'

Silence.

'Did you *have* to say that word in front of the boy?'

'Death! Death! Death! There! I've said it! It's out in the air. Try and take it back now, would you? Try and retract it now!'

'Now you're over-reacting and being infantile.'

'*I'm* being infantile?'

'Why can't we have an adult discussion about this?'

I walked out past the wolf and climbed the stairs to the second movement of the Cacophonie Hysteriata. The bride traipsed up with me, white gown billowing out behind her, wolf obediently in tow.

Once inside my bedroom, the first thing I noticed was that Patricia had vanished from her position upon the window ledge. I was feeling pretty on top of things so decided to give Caro a ring and meet her at a café somewhere, so as to discuss poor Patricia's mental health. I was still in my pyjamas, with a jersey slung casually over the top, so I opened my wardrobe to pull on some trousers. Princess Petal was swinging on the iron rail, hanging upside down by her legs, grinning like a loon. I screamed, then instantly regretted it, as I heard Red huffing and bounding up the staircase.

Bash, bash, bash.

'You all right, son?'

'Fine! Just got a bit of a fright. Be down and out shortly!'

'Right you are!'

Thump puff thump puff thump puff thud.

Pieces of leaf and bracken hung from her raven-coloured hair. In her right hand she clutched a brick.

'What's that?'

'Part of the palace wall.' She swung again, like a

monkey, then somersaulted off and into the middle of the floor. 'Sorry. I may have got some orange brick dust on a pair of your jeans.'

I took down a pair of blue jeans from a hanger, then moved to the oak dresser, holding in my breath before tugging on the handles of the second drawer.

Nothing came out at me.

Putting on a t-shirt, I shot Petal a last look in the mirror. She was irritating me, seeming a sort of spineless and pathetic creature, for ever locked in a world of childhood fantasy.

IX

KATE

Okay, so I lied about the head. Or rather, I remember now why I remembered. It was the face of the next-door neighbour's little boy as he was dressed up for Guy Fawkes night. What was his name again? Timmy or Johnny or Sonny-boy, or something similar. I only remember the mask because of what had happened between Maria and me that evening as we were getting ready to go out.

We'd been bickering about who got to wear what top, and she'd snatched something off me, so I'd whacked her one and her Mum'd come running up the stairs to see what was going on. By the time she entered the room we'd been rolling around on the floor, scratching and biting. I'm pretty ashamed about it now, but at the time . . . I just lost control. It wasn't just the top, it was all her little habits, the way she ate her hundreds and thousands sandwiches in little nibbles at a time, like a rabbit, and the way she picked at the skin around her cuticles. She never bloody stopped. Pick, pick, pick all day at school, pick, pick, pick all the way home, and after school too, on the trampoline or when we were playing Monopoly. Her hands were red and disgusting, all raw and bleeding around the nails. And I'd tried to talk her out of it too. You're not a kid any more, I told her, you've got to make your hands look nice. And I asked her why she did it, but she wouldn't say anything, she'd just stare straight ahead in a defiant sort of a way and pretend she hadn't heard. And there were other things she did, like turning her socks over at the top in one very neat fold – just one, nothing more and nothing less. Everything about her was always neat and perfect, except for the nails. That's why I just couldn't understand it.

I'm not making excuses for myself. I'm not proud of the fact that I left claw marks down her left cheek. But you can see that perhaps I had my reasons at the time. The fact that she wanted to wear the top that I wanted to wear just topped it all off. Sure we were at her house, and sure it was her top, but so bloody what? She was being a right pain, and years before we'd pricked fingers and rubbed our blood together and promised to be blood sisters and share everything for ever after. And now she was going back on her side of the bargain. Anyway, there we were, scrapping it down on the floor, and Maria's mother came in and started yelling at us and dragging us apart and I had to go to the carnival by myself.

It was getting late as I walked out through their front gate and the neighbours were beginning to set off fireworks in their back yards. No skyrockets yet, just sparklers and double happys and the odd Catherine wheel. The boy with the mask was jumping back and forth over the fence. He held a sparkler in his right hand, and gripped the fence with his left. Then he'd jump up and fling his legs over, first to one side, then to the next, and then back again. I was determined to go to the carnival without Maria, just to prove that I didn't need her as a friend.

I can't remember if it was cold that night, but I do know that I was so angry with Maria and I felt nauseous. Or perhaps that was due to the excess of candy floss which I had eaten. Either way, I was in a disgustingly bad mood. And I don't know how to tell about what happened next without sounding sentimental or trite. This is all I can reconstruct.

They were behind me, grabbing my hair, and holding my arms and then they were on top of me and forcing me down. They were calling out my name, Kate or Katherine, and there were two or three or four of them. They had a tape recorder with them. They were playing my favourite music.

We were amongst some straw, like in a barn, or in the quarters of one of the animals, and then two or three or one of them had my arms. I don't remember that. What I remember is Maria's head sliding around the edge of the building. What I remember is the look on her face. A look of horror, but also of something else. Something which might almost have been satisfaction. But she didn't say anything, do you understand, she didn't do anything, though they were on top of me, and loosening their belts. She was only there for an instant. And I was not screaming, don't you know, I never screamed. But I'm sure they saw her too. Because they paused, for an instant, and they froze, and I felt them look up, all two or three or four of them, and I felt like vomiting. I think I threw up. I don't know how long I was in there for. I forget. I have a memory like a strobe light. Full glare, flicker, half-light, flicker, flicker, blackout.

I black out, I lose my memory. I close my eyes at night, and I don't see those four figures, I never saw those four figures. I never saw Maria's face watching. When I close my eyes at night, there is only black. I close my eyes and I am falling, falling, over the edge of a cliff, or from the railing of a bridge, or in an elevator shaft, falling and falling and never hitting the bottom of anything. And my emptiness washes over me like the ocean, and I become my own emptiness. That's all that I become.

When I think of the carnival now, I see the lights of the carousel revolving. In the space where I fell down, where I was pushed, there is only the darkness, closing in over my head, red and black. Ink and blood. Purple flowers. I don't remember anything. The next day it snowed, and I stayed in my room. All day and all night I watched the snow come down, and in the morning, when I wiped the pane and looked out, I could see the tracks of animals. I climbed over the window ledge and on to the lawn and began to build statues out of snow and ice. Women and men on horseback. I gave them plaques of ice which bore no names. I didn't feel cold at all, although I could see my fingers turning purple and my breath was frozen before it left my mouth.

Of course I never told nobody. And I never spoke to Maria again.

Some things are better left unsaid.

X

Jim

I caught her on the telephone in my room. No. Not *her*, not my ice-cream angel. I don't even have her telephone number. How on earth would I call her? No. Not her. Just old Caro. She had just got out of bed, and agreed to take time out to come and meet me in downtown Melbourne.

I made sure the door was securely guarded, then took the silver ladder which Steven had installed for me out of the bedroom window. Looking in the kitchen window, I could see Mum sitting at the table with her head in her hands whilst Red rubbed her back. Willy would be in the lounge, rolling in front of the TV, watching *Mash* re-runs. Or perhaps he would be absent. Perhaps he would be elsewhere. They could say the word 'dead'; it meant nothing. Some of us had lives to lead.

I ran downtown and caught the shuttle to the airport. I was in time for the 10:15 flight, so would be able to make the three o'clock deadline at the Melbourne café. I don't remember much about the flight, except the free drinks and the cloud of halitosis coming from the mouth of the man sitting next to me, his meal tray rising and falling with each breath he took. The flickering of an in-flight movie. The safety instructions tucked into the back pocket of the seat in front of me.

What else can I say? I believe I had a couple of G and Ts and passed out, because the next thing I remember is the Melbourne International Airport, coming down the metal steps, clack, clack, clack on to the tarmac, and heading for the waiting area. An airport just like any other, people busily waving and attempting to locate baggage and relatives. Grandmothers waving gifts from Hawaii, fathers looking slightly nervous at all the overt emotion, mothers demonstrating the hula . . .

No, it deserves more than this. I shall describe this airport for you, then whenever I say 'airport' you may summon this mental image in your mind. Elsewhere you may find descriptions of bus stops or railway stations. I shall describe the airport.

There is a desk like any other, positioned against the far wall. The tellers wear high heels, and their blue uniforms are all very smart. The Customs desks are further on, sniffer dogs and all. The plastic waiting chairs are blue in colour, and are to be found in the middle of the main lounge, just to the right of the cafeteria.

Nature of the cafeteria? Impersonal, efficient. Slightly stale coffee, scones just a touch on the crumbling side, the butter on the blueberry muffins in hard dobs. Businessmen rustling newspapers. Bored serving ladies.

'No, *push* the button. Can't you read the sign?'

The carpet in the general area is geometrically patterned, so as to hide cigarette butts, coffee stains, flecks of potato crisps and the odd discreet pile of chunder. Travel sickness does not always time itself around conveniently placed paper sickbags.

Nature of the geometric pattern upon the carpet? Large, so as to convey a feeling of distortion of perspective. This is the carpet also found in hospital and hotel foyers. There also it mingles with the scent of over-heated pies and Jeyes cleaning fluid. A stooped man is always cleaning, earning money to support his wife and family.

This, of course, is a reconstruction. The real airport, far off in time and space, contains all these details and more. The clocks show not one time, but many, the times of all major cities around the globe. LA, London, Paris, Milan, Swedenborg, Siberia.

Time passing. Another shuttle.

Melbourne. The boulevard was jostling with women in bright primary colours and men in hats and scarves. I ordered a cappuccino and sat down outside under a red and white striped umbrella. Small bowls of brown coffee sugar sat crusting in the centre of the tables next to glass ashtrays. I took out my cigar and lit it, then turned nonchalantly to the second page of the paper. Kylo brought my coffee. He'd cleaned up his act, cut his hair and got a job as a waiter. Said it was the shock of all those body parts, the sight of a human reduced to sections of flesh and vein. Every guy's gotta settle down and try and get himself a decent wage and a crime-free lifestyle eventually.

I felt Caro's hand on my shoulder, and then she was sitting down opposite me.

'God, I just negotiated the most hectic rush-hour traffic! My alarm didn't ring, and being exhausted from last night's seminar, I slept till twelve! Would you believe it? Twelve o'clock. Then, when I got out on the motorway, I found myself stuck in the centre lane and missed the turn-off, so I had to do a U turn and just about got myself arrested. Then parking! Shit, I might as well have walked, though that would have been a laugh in these heels.' She bent down and adjusted one of her shoes, then pulled back the chiffon scarf which she had tied around her neatly coiled red hair. I sucked on my cigar. 'Anyway, enough about me. What do you think of Patricia?'

I blew a thin stream of smoke across the table.

'Seriously,' she recomposed her face, 'lucky you rang. I'm bloody worried about her. She's had a bout of this before, when Bertie ran off over here with that twat from the office. She convinced herself that he'd been wrestling sharks on the Gold Coast, and nobody could tell her otherwise. Gary rang me to tell me about the fantasies she'd been indulging in, but being stuck over here, what could I do? I wrote her a letter saying that if she felt like getting away from it all, Gary and I would pay for the fare and she could come over after the course has finished. Spend a week together looking around the shops and going to a couple of shows. She never replied.'

'She'd been writing you letters. Gary found them crumpled up in a heap behind the dresser, a whole series of them. Including reports of your behaviour at the supposed circus, and a couple of fairy tales relayed by a Russian guy.'

'*Fairy tales*! That *is* odd. Do you think it's some return-to-childhood thing? Shit. Shit. I should have gone round to see her more often after Bertie died. Still, you'd think she would have got over that by now. That was at least three years ago.'

'Post-traumatic stress syndrome.'

'Is that what they're calling it?' She bit her bottom lip nervously and toyed with one corner of her headscarf. 'When was the last sighting?'

'The shrink at the home talked to her two days ago. Said she'd displayed very aggressive qualities, then apparently gone back to her bedroom, packed her bags and disappeared somewhere.'

'She can't have gone too far. She didn't have any transport.'

'Perhaps she's gone bush.'

'What would she live off? Huhu grubs and supplejack?'

'All right. Maybe she's gone to stay with somebody out on the coast or in some small central town.'

I caught Kylo's eye and he came over, bending his head slightly sideways so that he might fit under the umbrella which sheltered our table.

'How long?'

'You'd better run.'

'Thanks.'

'Who's that?'

'Kylo. Got a mutual friend of ours to visit. Can I see you again?'

'You're running away already?'

'Sorry. Got a million things to do. When shall we meet again?'

'Just let me check my diary. Wouldn't want to stand anybody else up. Yes . . . mmm . . . hang on . . . '

'Later tonight?'

'No. I have to leave the country. What about night after tomorrow? Here? For dinner?'

'I guess so. We need some sort of plan of action.'

'What can we do?'

'Try and get in contact with her?'

'Yes. I suppose so. Put notices over the radio, and in the newspapers. Get on to national television.'

I nodded briskly, stubbed out my cigarette and left the café to catch the downtown shuttle.

Planes, airports, planes, airports, planes, airports.

XI

KATE

Despite the agoraphobia that he later fell prey to, my father was a very fair man. He always divided everything up equally between my brother and I. If Damon had a toy train set, then so did I. This meant that Damon was also given Barbie dolls and Russian dolls and fluffy toy dogs and other things that he didn't like at all. But it was great for me, because I got to play with robots and matchbox cars. Even when we were given gifts from other people, we still had to share. For instance, my mother had a friend who owned a hat shop and when I turned ten she gave me a gigantic box of brightly coloured feathers. They were mangey, bedraggled things that had fallen out of hats or been plucked from the nether regions of dead birds. But they were feathers all the same. And I had to share them with my brother, which I wasn't happy about at all. His friends used to tease him, because they once opened up his wardrobe and found a Barbie and Ken dinner set. When they caught him playing with some feathers they gave him shit about it for weeks afterwards. This was when I had just made friends with Maria, and we would play in my bedroom and my brother and his friends would come raging into the room and stomp on whatever we were doing.

I'm sure my brother only wanted half those feathers

to spite me, just to try and have as much as I had. That was what really got me. He didn't want them for their own sake, he only wanted them to spite me. If you look at a photograph of us at around this time, you'll see that my brother has a handful of feathers and he's sticking them together with mud and wax. And I'm there, next to him and slightly behind, waving to the camera.

Shortly after that, I stole all my brother's feathers and put them with my own in the cardboard box which they had come in. I went down to the river at the back of our section and dug a hole in the mud with an iron pole, just near the little wooden plank bridge, and I buried the feathers down there, about a foot deep. If I couldn't have them all, then I didn't want to have any. It's not that I was selfish about them, it's just that it disgusted me, the way he coated the turquoise ones in mud, and smeared the yellow ones with the blood from his scabby knee and plunged the red ones into wax.

I didn't like that bridge so much, because that was where my brother nearly drowned. We were playing at the river, on a Saturday, as we used to when I was about ten, when he was about twelve, down by the water, under the bridge. Maria wouldn't come down near the river with us. She said it gave her the creeps. And my brother's friends used to play rugby on Saturdays while Damon, who was an asthmatic, was forced to play with his sister. I think that we'd just discovered crocodiles, although my brother was just beginning to grow out of animal games and to some extent he considered them juvenile. He was into crocodiles because he'd read, in a nature book somewhere, about how they kill their victims. He said they come and sneak up on you as you lie sunbathing and reading your book and sipping your iced coffee. They sneak up out of the mud and grab you in their jaws.

Then they take you down in that slow white drown called a death roll, and they turn you over and over and over until they feel you stop struggling. Then they take you to their lair and they hang you up and you start to rot and when you stink enough they eat you.

We had to pretend we lived in Australia. I wasn't sure if crocociles could smell underwater or not, but my brother said they must or they wouldn't know when their food was ripe. Unless they went by sight. Anyway, that's what we were playing at that day. And I'm not sure whether I was playing the crocodile or the victim, but somehow I was out of the water and my brother was in, and then he must have got his legs caught in something like green weed, and we both screamed and panicked and thought that maybe a crocodile had swum here from Australia, or come over hidden in a packing case, like the tigersnakes had a couple of years ago. Turned out it was only a piece of weed, and we both felt kind of stupid that our overactive imaginations had caused us so much panic.

He reckons he passed out through fear, but he never passed out like I did.

XII

Jim

England. Strangeways. Winter. No leaves on the stark black boughs. The fence stretched around the grounds, the top five lines of wire electrified.

A guard met me at the gate, walky-talky in hand, mid-calf black boots spit-polished to perfection, navy uniform neatly pressed. He escorted me to the visitors' entrance, where I was shown into a green-painted anteroom. I flicked through a couple of women's magazines to pass the time. Shortly a warden appeared, in the same immaculate outfit as the guard, and asked me who I was here to see. I told him. He took me out of the room and down through the main cell block. Most of the prisoners were quiet, some sleeping, some writing letters home or to their beautiful girlfriends, some giving me the eye, whistling and cat-calling as I walked past. I became acutely aware of the tightness of my jeans.

'Hey, pretty boy! Come spend a night in *my* hole.'

'Why don't you just paint them trousers on!'

Ringer's cell was the ninth on the left. He was sitting on his bed with his head between his hands. I expected that we might stop, so I could talk to him then and there through the cell bars, but the guard merely motioned toward him with a flick of his wrist and raised his eyebrows as if to say, 'This the one?' Ringer didn't look up. I nodded, and followed the guard through a right turn and into the visitors' room. There I sat at a desk inside a small booth and stared through a pane of glass that stretched from the desk up to the ceiling. On the other side of the glass Ringer came through, escorted by the uniformed guard. He stared right through me.

'Hey man! It's me!'

'What are you doing here?'

'Come to see how you are, boyo.'

'What the fuck would you care, bastard?'

'Cool it! I'm here to help.'

'You call that helping! You call that . . . that . . . making me kill my Pop, then zooming away in your car, you call that helping? I'd like to see your hindering then, Sunshine. Yes, I'd really like to see that.'

'What? You're all mixed up. You're all, like, confused, your brain's playing tricks on you! That wasn't me made you do all that! That was Kylo.'

'Don't you pull those bloody sweet tricks with me, mate! Don't you go on and pretend to be somebody you're not. Sure enough I know who you are and why you're here, you two-timing pimp.'

'Hey, I never pimped on you.'

'Sure you heard about my case. You were testifying in the witness box. Yeah, I saw him put the spade into his Pop. No, his Pop never did nothing to deserve it. Yeah, he had intent. No, his Pop never made him chop wood till four in the morning just for being out with a babe. No, sir, we never egged him on, and I was never there at the bridge. I don't know how he got out there, sir, I guess he just hitch-hiked with the body stuffed into a sack. Yes, sir, the accused quite often displayed violent tendencies before the murder. Yes, I would say that he had the mind and disposition of a hardened criminal. Yes your honour, no your honour, yes jury, no jury, anything you want me to say, only I am innocent and this man is guilty. Of the murder. And I had nothing to do with it. No, sir, I never drove the car, supplied the spade, egged him on, sang like a fucking canary with each blow of the instrument. Yes, sir, your honour sir, a violent man. Guilty, guilty, guilty, yes this man is guilty, does he have anything more to confess?'

'That wasn't me! You remember me? From the Big Girl's Arms! I stole those jeans for you!'

'I don't wanna know about you and your petty crime rings! Why don't you just fuck off, squealer!'

'Hey! I know how you killed your old man, but it doesn't matter to me. I wanna help you get out of here.'

'You can help me. *You* can get *your* arse out of this place before I count to three. Now, I'm gonna close my eyes and do this really slowly. By the time I open my eyes, I don't wanna see your ugly face behind this fucking sheet of glass. Do you hear me!'

'It would be hard not to.'

'Shut up! Are you ready . . . one . . . two . . . two and a half . . . two and three-quarters . . . '

I pushed back my chair and motioned to the guard, who unlocked a door between the two rooms, then quickly escorted me out into the cell block.

'He's pretty far gone, isn't he?'

'I don't know what you mean.'

I sighed. 'He didn't used to be like that. I don't understand it.'

'Prison can change a man. What your friend has done is a terrible thing. Murder is one of the most cold-blooded crimes a man can commit. But murder of one's own father? A man shudders.' He shuddered.

'He's not a violent type. He just lost control. It's Kylo that's really the bad egg of the group.'

'Kylo?'

'The ringleader. He's working at a café in Melbourne now. Went to another country and straightened out his act.'

'Our laws still apply over the ocean.'

'Yes, of course.'

We were moving through the cell block now, the same hands reaching out from behind the bars, the same cat-calls and jeers.

'If it were found that he had lied in the witness box?'

'False evidence?'

'Yes. It would affect Ringer's sentence.'

'If he was wrongly accused . . . '

'A re-trial?'

'Perhaps.'

We were back in the anteroom.

'Could Kylo be arrested and tried over there, do you think?'

'Certainly.'

I wrote the name and address of the Melbourne café on a scrap of paper found in one corner of my jeans pocket.

'Look to it,' I said with an air both authoritative and dismissive at once. He nodded. I seemed to carry some weight with these prison wardens. The gate guard showed me to the exit, then stood on sentry behind me.

And the tedious journey home.

Planes, airports, planes, airports.

Up the drainpipe and into the bedroom.

Bash, bash, bash.

'Son? Are you in there?'

'I'm sleeping.'

'Come on down for dinner now, like a good boy.'

Down the staircase, tightly gripping the wooden banister. I sat myself at the kitchen table. Mother thrust a plate of peas, bangers and mash under my nose. I reached for the salt and the tomato sauce, smothering the plate with both.

'Nice day at the beach?'

'Oh, yes. We had a lovely little walk along the promenade. And we stopped in at that little ice-cream shop and bought a vanilla snow-freeze each. You should have come.'

Ice-cream shop? The waves breaking gently against the shore, the gulls crying lonely utterances to the wind. Her blonde hair obscuring her face and flicking its ends into her grey-green eyes as she reaches to pick up various sea shells from the sand: conch, paua, cockle. Her pastiche floral skirt flapping around her coltish legs, tones of red, yellow, dusky orange . . .

I shovelled in a few more peas and a bit of mash.

'We're here for each other, Jimmy. As a family.'

I speared open my sausage, mushed some peas into the crevasse, then topped it all off with another squirt of blood-red sauce.

'We really do think it'd be good for you to come on a drive with us tomorrow.'

'Too busy.'

'Oh, Jim.' Disappointed, wary Mother.

Shovel peas, gulp water.

'Leave him alone, eh, love. You'll only upset him further.'

'He needs to get it all out in the open. It's only healthy.'

'All in good time.'

Rise. Move to sink. Scrape remains of meal into

scrap bucket. Rinse plate. Stack plate. Parental eyes boring holes into backbone.

'Where you off to tonight, son?'

'Going to see Timmo. Then to the pub.'

'Good boy.'

'But he's spent all afternoon at the pub!'

'You go on along, son. I'll look after your mother. You go and visit some of those friends of yours.'

Loosen belt, head down corridor, out past the front room, out through the front door and into the street.

XIII

KATE

Today, a disturbing thing happened. It was getting near closing time at the dairy (8 p.m.) and this really weedy, scrawny-looking bloke walked in, asking for goody-goody gumdrops ice-cream. I told him to piss off, 'cause I was mopping the floor and I'd shut the ice-cream freezer up for the night, and put the scoops and the cones away and I didn't want to get the whole lot back out again. But after I'd told him to naff off, he just stood there and stared at me, all googly-eyed, only he wasn't looking right *at* me exactly, but at something just behind my shoulder. He had something that looked like a paintbrush sticking out of his back pocket. This staring went on for a minute or two, with me just sort of looking back at him, bemused, and then I had to yell out, Oi mate are you all right¿, and then he looked me straight on, like I was a Martian or something. Enough to send shivers right down your spine.

I mean, he wasn't exactly the kind of guy you want hanging around after hours. Especially not in the winter, when it's pitch black by 7.30 and you have to walk home on your own after work. I'm not saying he seemed like an attacker or anything, but he *did* look a bit funny in the eye and he stared at me in an odd sort of way. You notice that kind of guy. Actually, you notice anyone under fifty. I work in a retirement area, a lot of nice houses with well-kept gardens. The biggest excitement was when they put a new gutter in on the waterfront road. Most of the residents had been waiting fifteen years for that. Caused a real stir. And this guy who was in the shop was the kind of degenerate that would write his initials in the wet cement. Not that you can necessarily tell that sort of thing about somebody first off. But I could tell with this guy. Well, he was standing all over my clean floor, wasn't he? And not a sign of an apology. You could bet that if he wrote his initials in that cement he wouldn't wipe them out in a hurry. Well, you can't have those kind of people around. So I had to go and get the lady who manages the place to shove him out the door. But she couldn't convince him to leave, so she had to go on and get her husband to come and talk to him. But he just hung around inside the door, his mouth hanging open like he was about to catch flies or something. So one of my bosses grabbed a broom and the other one grabbed a smelly old mop and they chased him off. And I cleaned up and went home.

I was happy that I hadn't encouraged that guy. If you let that kind of person hang around once, they just keep coming back, like a memory you don't want returning. Maria used to tell me to get rid of people like that quick smart or you'd live to regret it. Maria used to tell me a lot of things, and most of those things have stuck, despite the carnival. Maria herself has stuck. You can try and try to get somebody like Maria out of your head, but once they're in there, they're in there, and there's not much you can do about it. She's still around. I've even kept my photos of her.

Here she is in one, looking darker than she is in real life, and a good deal smaller. She is what my mother would call 'big-boned'. This photo was taken on the day we became blood sisters. It was her idea: she stole a pin from her mother's sewing-room drawer and pricked her finger, like Sleeping Beauty. Only she was Sleeping Beauty *and* the witch, because she then held *my* hand down, palm upwards, and stabbed the needle into my forefinger. I watched as the blood formed a small, round globule. She rubbed our fingers together, and then we were bonded for life, she said, and whatever happened to me would happen to her as well, and whatever happened to her would also be happening to me. Better than being twins, she said. Now you are my double.

It was soon after this photo was taken that Dad got sick. It all started when Mum mentioned that the family should go on a holiday together, maybe down to Wainakau, and then Dad went all quiet, and the next day he didn't go to work. Damon stood in for him and told the staff that Dad'd just got a bad case of the flu. Dad was in his study at home, holed up like some kind of cave-creature. He was sleeping in there, so poor old Mum was left to cuddle up into the empty air where he used to sleep. It must've been kind of cold in the study too, since the radiator in that room was on the blink and Mum won't allow fan heaters in the house 'cause they use up so much electricity. Anyway, Mum was forced to pass Dad's meals in through the window, 'cause he wouldn't open the door. Mum was a nervous wreck – she aged about ten years in those ten days. And there was a nasty stench coming from the room. Well, Dad'd been pissing and crapping in the pot plants, hadn't he? Disgusting. We just about puked when we got into the room. But I'll spare you the gory details.

Damon was the hero of the hour. Damon's the hero of every bloody hour. He was the one who talked Dad into coming out. Stood outside the door and talked for four hours solid. I wouldn't have thought there was much point in talking to a closed door. It worked, though. Dad came out, went straight to the bathroom, took a shower, got into some clean clothes and we all went on as if nothing had happened.

It turned out it wasn't just that first idea of going on holiday that had triggered him off, either. There was another factor involved. One of the the rival carpet factories had put an ad on TV for a new shagpile they'd just put out, and the wife of Dad's best friend was in it. She was dressed in this long slinky black number, sort of lolling around on the shagpile and flashing her cleavage. Dad sat very quietly watching the ad. Then he went to the telephone and tried to dial Marty's number. We watched him listening to the continued ring. Then he muttered 'Traitor' under his breath, and went upstairs and locked himself into his study.

If you ask me, Dad's just too spoilt. He knows that Mum's gonna bring his meals up to the room, and he knows that Damon's gonna take over his job at the carpet factory, and he knows that we'll stand outside the door and try to talk to him.

And he also knows that when he comes out, for the sake of keeping the hurricane calm, we'll all pussyfoot around him for the next six months. It's like walking up a volcanic slope. Not only does the scree mean that it's two steps forward and one step back, but there's always the knowledge of the impending explosion.

XIV

JIM

I was feeling pretty good for the first three blocks. Then it hit me. The sickness, the disease, the illness, the nausea. I felt it rising up through the soles of my feet, setting my head spinning and the sidewalk rotating up to meet my vision. I saw a series of cracks start out from the sidewalk and split infinitely, like the roots of a tree, so that I felt myself to be leaping and jumping on an ice plateau, abysses opening up on every side of me. Things existed separately from their names, and names hung before me like blank sheets of cardboard. Nameless things and thingless names. A blank space seemed to surround my head, flooding my eyes with a nothingness of overwhelming intensity. A painful white light moved in through my forehead and I felt as if I might vomit, so moved towards a nearby rubbish tin most hastily. Jumping cracks with skill and dexterity, I leaned my head over the edge of the metal and peered down at an empty waste of milk cartons and chicken carcasses. Concentrating fixedly on a partially fly-blown ribcage, I found the existential seasickness passing as quickly as it came, and I could continue calmly towards Timmo's front door.

A few swift slaps about the face and head saw him wide awake.

'What the hell are you doing here?'

'What?'

'How did you escape?'

'What the fuck are you on about?'

'How did you get out?'

'Why are you here?'

'On the off-chance that you'd get out! And you have. Shit, you'd better not be seen out and about. You must be one of the country's most wanted men.'

'What the hell are you on, mate? Look, a bloke just needs a decent night's kip all right, or he gets all edgy.'

'Okay, okay. Meet me later though? At the Big Girl? Better chuck on a wig or something, lest the bluebells get after you.'

'Bluebells?'

'You're right. Better give up the lingo too, or they'll be after us twice as quick.'

'What time?'

'Ten. Give me time to get to Melbourne, fix up some business and come back to drink myself silly.'

'Are you a nightmare?'

'No. I'm a pleasant Sunday afternoon fantasy. Get some more sleep. Dream a bit. See you at ten.'

Timmo snuffled back down into the softness of the white pillow and I stealthily crept out the front door.

XV

Kate

Here I am in my bedroom, getting ready for a night out with the girls. Suppose we'll be drinking at the Big Girl's Arms. For a change.

God, the blokes that drink there are revolting, and thick as pigshit, most of them. Still, beggars can't be choosers, I suppose. Not that my friends and I ever have to try much with the fellas that go there. Like flies to sticky honey, they are. For one night, anyway. One shag and they're gone. Getting a screw's one thing, getting a fella to stay around is totally different. It doesn't actually affect me much, but sometimes Michelle, my main drinking mate, gets a bit upset about the fact that she doesn't have a boyfriend. Last week she gave me a bit of a fright. Started talking about trying to get herself up the duff on purpose, just so that she might get some bloke to move in with her. Scared me shitless, that did. She came right, though. I gave her a picture I had stashed away in my undies drawer of this woman giving birth and the head coming out all slimy and yoghurty, and she just about chucked. And then I raved on a bit about morning sickness, and getting cut open and sewn up, and about kids squealing and screaming all day and all night, and I kept on going until she promised me that she'd stay on the pill. Shit, I really love Michelle, but sometimes she can come up with the weirdest plans.

Now, bit of mascara but only on the top lashes, otherwise it'll run and I'll look like that chick from the Addams Family, and just a touch of eyeliner, bit of hairspray, plenty of lippy, and there! I hate getting dressed up to go out. You know, is this pink top too slutty or these jeans too tight? If you dress in nice stuff then you're a slut or a prickteaser, and if you wear baggy stuff then you're a frumpy old cow. Fuck them. Who needs to score? It's only ever revolting blokes and freaks that want to shag me anyway. Give me a freak and he'll fall in love with me the minute he sets eyes on me.

Speaking of freaks and losers, I saw that bloke the other day, you know the one in the ice-cream shop. It was at the Big Girl, wasn't it. By God, he's right fucking creepy. I think he might fancy me too, what with the way he was acting and all. I was standing in the pub talking to some equally sleazy-looking fella, and he came up to me smoking a pencil real cool and casual. He didn't talk at me neither, he talked to my breasts. That's the kind of man I really like. One that can't take his eyes off your cleavage. And dumb old me went and spilt the beans about my moniker.

'Kate,' he repeats, like a scratched record, 'Kate, Kate, Kate', as if the name was part of some kinky sex fantasy he liked to play out at home. Anyway, he kind of ruined my night really, 'cause he kept staring, all googly-eyed, and it made me want to vomit. Have you ever had that? When someone just won't get the hint? And he wasn't just sleazy either. Like I said, he had something right creepy about him, sort of a maniacal gleam in his eye. Made me want to run a fucking mile, that did, made me want to run a fucking mile.

We didn't stay long, me and Michelle. We left after

our second drink. We'd like to find a different watering hole. But in a town like this, there's nowhere else to go.

XVI

JIM

Shuttle airport plane airport shuttle. By my new watch I figured that I'd be just in time.

The lights were on inside and lit up the clean café like a great yellow lamp. The golden glare spilled out on to the street, stretching the shadows of the power poles into a series of diagonal parallel stripes. Kylo was nowhere in sight, so I ordered carrot cake and cappuccino from another waiter. Rain began to splatter against the outside of the windows, creating a hazy curtain of yellow light upon the pane.

'Where's Kylo?'

'Kylo? Haven't you heard? He's been arrested for giving false evidence at the trial of the bloke who did his father in with a spade last year.'

'No. I hadn't heard.'

'Apparently he's going on trial himself now. If he's guilty, the other guy could walk.'

Caro arrived flushed and panting, as the day before.

'Sorry. I'm a little late.'

'No excuses necessary.'

'Quite. Have you heard anything?'

'Yes. She was perched on my window ledge this morning. Then she disappeared when I went down to have breakfast.'

'Shit. You should never have let her get away that easily. Were you nice to her?'

'I may have asked where the hell she'd been.'

'Could you do something to lure her back? Perhaps leave a trail of crumbs on the ledge or something?'

'She's not a bloody Java sparrow!'

'No. You're right.'

'Have you been in touch with Gary or the shrink?'

'I talked to Gary on the phone after you and I parted. He says no one's heard anything about her and the whole Street is dead worried. The part that I find bloody creepy is the fact that she chose *me* of all people to "write" to. I'm hardly a glamourpuss!'

'But you'd gone overseas. She's hardly been out of the house in twenty years.'

'Still. It's kind of spooky. At least she doesn't have a violent streak, or I'd expect her to come bursting in here with a machete.'

'Hardly. The most she'd do is poison your fish.'

'Do you think she'll come again?'

'Dunno. What am I going to do if she does? God knows how she gets up to the ledge. I suppose she shimmies up the pear tree with that old gaberdine frock hitched up around her waist.'

'She'll ladder her stockings!'

'Oh crying shame!'

We laughed briefly, then fell silent. A full moon hung against the black sky like a white paper circle cut out and patched against a theatrical backdrop of night. The seas and craters lay as if etched upon the surface by some prank cartographer. I couldn't believe that the moon and the sky were real, but felt rather that if I sliced across the sky with a pen-knife it would split open like an egg and I would be sucked out into the vacuum of outer space.

'Jimmy! Did you hear me?'

'Hmm?'

'I wish you'd learn to listen. It's damn frustrating.'

'Sorry.'

'I was telling you that next time she appears you should throw a sheet over her and wrestle her to the floor.'

'That sounds like excellent advice.'

'What do you suggest then?'

'No sarcasm. I'll do it.'

'Great. You don't have to rush off again, do you?'

''Fraid so. Busy, busy. Got to keep on the move or the big inertia'll sneak up and grab me from behind.'

'There doesn't seem much point . . . '

'What?'

'There doesn't seem much point to you coming all the way over here just for a five-minute chat every second day. It's getting a bit ridiculous, don't you think? How in hell are you affording it?'

'When my father died I came into a small inheritance.'

'That's convenient.'

'Yes. My father always wanted me to travel.'

'It seems so extravagant. Why can't you just phone?'

How could I tell her I had nothing else to do? All this time. Time on my hands. They say it's like that when somebody dies. Space and time collapse. There's just a hole, as black as can be. Only it isn't in outer space. It sits in the middle of your chest like a concrete slab, and can't be coughed up. I conveyed my thoughts with a casual shrug of the shoulders.

'All right. Have it your way. I won't travel any more. I'll try and catch you on the telephone. Or you can phone me.' I handed over my home phone number. 'Call me.'

She nodded. The rain had ceased. The street lamps were dimming and the sun began to shine through the spaces between the poles. As the sun was rising I moved out into the lines of shadow and headed for the shuttle which would take me to the eternal airport, which I have already described.

But, oh yes, the airport toilets.

This is where you find me after seeing Caro. Standing before the cracked looking glass which glints a shade of grey above the wash stand, nervously pulling back my sleeve to examine Mr Tick-Tock. The seconds hand has stopped. Removing the watch from my wrist, I beat it upon the side of the sink until it resumes ticking, then move towards the urinal and relieve myself. Just for fun I sign my name in urine, enjoying the sight of the yellow streams trickling down the iron wall, in and out of time with each other. Ah, Harmony.

XVII

KATE

Michelle dropped me home in her car. We were both pretty pissed off that we'd had to cut our night short just 'cause of some bastard with googly eyes, but none of us wanted to stay in there. It was like being under surveillance from the secret police. Constantly, we are watched.

I didn't go straight to bed. I walked up the stairs and yelled out Goodnight, I'm in the house, to Dad so that he wouldn't think I'd been out too late. Then I lay on my bed and stared up at the ceiling, only I don't like to be in my room much. So I went out the window for a walk along the beach. It's amazing what you can find down there. They have those sea tulips, do you know the ones? They look all worn and shrivelled, like a bunch of dead mice. Well, imagine that. Imagine being given something that looked as if it's been caught in a rat trap. All pink and white and that. Like mice with young babies suckling. Perhaps it's that I'm morbid, but I actually quite like that sort of thing. I've never been one for roses and red wine.

They're like the mice in the straw at the carnival. They're like all the things I don't want to remember.

XVIII

JIM

'Harmony,' I said, 'that's the key. The novel should be as delicately orchestrated as a Bach symphony.'

Larkin was picking at his teeth with an old match. Timmo sat with a set of handcuffs around his left wrist. Buckell had his nose buried in a book. He looked up suddenly.

'Listen, old thing. We're frightfully sorry about what's happened. With the brother and all. Mother sends her regards. And we do hope you're all right about the whole thing. After all, it can't be too easy to deal with, being the second death in the nuclear family and all that. Still, at least you're still of sound body and mind yourself, eh? Never underestimate the virtue of that, eh Jimmo.'

I gazed out the bar window. Beyond the high-rise buildings, the blue outlines of the cardboard cut-out mountains rose majestically in the west.

'So you're coping all right?'

'Yes.'

The table began to spin as if on a rotating pedestal. I felt that morning's porridge swimming in a vast ocean of Guinness and red wine. Petal and the bride were walking hand and hand along the main street. Petal's right hand held the leash to which the wolf was reluctantly attached.

'I'm so glad you're out of prison, Timmo. How lucky that I had that chat with the prison warden. I think you owe me a drink or two for that. I guess Kylo'll soon be the one behind bars. Still, you are guilty, aren't you?'

Dust was blowing up from the road in small whirlpools, slowly circling the trio as they approached the pub. Petal tied the wolf to a pole outside and entered the bar with the bride following, the tatters of her train rustling softly after them. I saw the bride order two pints of Guinness, then take a table towards the rear of the Big Girl.

'I mean, you put the spade in, after all, and for that there can be no forgiveness. You may have escaped the long arm of the law this time, Ringer, but you may not be so lucky in the future.'

I turned to Kylo. 'Why aren't you in court?' I looked at Mr Tick Tock. 'Your hearing was meant to be at this time! You'll be holding up the judge!' Then, lowering the tone of my voice to one of coy conspiracy, I added, 'I hear he doesn't like to be kept waiting.'

Monty tugged on a lock of Kylo's hair. 'You listening to what he's saying?'

Kylo looked up from his book. 'Just his usual rambling, isn't it?'

''Course, we'll come and visit you, if you do end up in the clink. I always pay visits to my friends. Wouldn't leave you in there all alone with your bread and water, would we, boys?'

Ringer and Monty gave small, tentative shakes of the head.

Outside, the wolf pushed a disconsolate paw across a matted muzzle. Feeling the red wine starting to rise, I humbly excused myself, ran to the toilet and threw up in full view of myself in the full-length mirror. When I arrived back at the table, Buckell was polishing off the last of his pint.

'You all right, boyo?'

'Yes.'

I wiped the last traces of puke from the corners of my mouth.

'What were you talking about?'

'When?'

'Before. Just before.'

I searched the dim nooks and crags of memory, but came up with only a small chink of blank space where before had rested sound.

'I have forgotten.'

'So quickly?'

'Yes. Bloody Mnemosyne.' The bride swayed across the room, looking a little tiddly on her feet. 'Excuse me.'

I took her arm and led her outside to help untie the wolf. Petal ran out after us, all pink chiffon and high heels. She seemed to have adopted the role of nursemaid, or lady-in-waiting, to the bride. She took the former's arm and led her away, murmuring gentle admonishments. The bride paused to throw up in a shop doorway before continuing on down the street. I went back to the boys.

'Who would have thought that the old blind lady might spin the earth upside down and put one of you in prison and the other free? And now what will happen? Ah, but who can remember the future?'

Kylo's hair dropped from his head on to the table, where it landed in a small, neat pile. His face dripped away like melting yellow butter. His features fell into each other: he was collapsing, exploding, falling apart before my very eyes. I found myself staring at a smaller and smaller pile of Kylo. He was deconstructing, that's what it was. Goddam. I'd heard about this. It's not the Kylo, it's the space where Kylo wasn't – more specifically, the space where he no longer was. I watched this gap very closely. Kylo was only defined by not-Kylo, which in this case actually equalled Buckell. I watched Buckell making up. A fine blend of chromosomes and cells. A pretty clockwork toy. I saw the wind-up mechanism inserted into his backbone, the screw that makes the pretty ballerina sitting inside the music-box dance in time to the pretty tune.

By the time Kylo had exploded and remade himself as Buckell, I was feeling pretty dizzy in my head.

Then she entered.

My little ice-cream lady. She clutched a cone in one hand, and a small red purse in the other. Two friends were with her, not as equals, but as a black background against which the star may shine. My little Stella. I wiped the dribble away from my chin with the back of my hand. God, she was gorgeous. Dressed all in black, with long blonde hair cascading down her back, not dead straight, but falling in soft waves. She headed up to the bar and ordered a pint of cider. So did Buckell. Bastard. I watched him standing casually beside her, one elbow leaning on the bar, the other on his hip in an open pose, inviting speech. I could smell the puke on my own breath. Shit. Shit shit shit. I tried to catch her eye, but she was oblivious. She was so familiar. I must have met her some time before. I had to know her name. I searched the shelves of memory once more, but found only empty glass jars without labels. Damn this. This stupid little post-adolescent crush. She was chatting to Buckell. Or rather, she talked to his face while he talked to her breasts. He was bringing her over to our corner table. Keep calm old boy keep calm act cool she doesn't want you slobbering all over her like an excited puppy. Deep breaths now, deep breaths. Cigarette. That's cool. Ultra-smooth. I swigged my cider. God, she was almost here. I reached into my pocket, my eyes still fixed upon her perfect voluptuous form, and took out a solid-seeming cigarette, which I placed in my mouth. Strange taste, must be the stomach acid. Then she was opposite me, her eyes opposite mine, light bright blue, almost translucent. I held my lighter casually up to my cigarette. There was a smell of burning wood and lead.

'Do you usually smoke your pencils?' she asked.

Buckell laughed for far longer than was either necessary or polite.

'Poor little Jim, always trying so hard to impress.'

She ignored him, God bless her, and held out her hand. Small, freckled, wearing three rings.

'Kate.'

I believe I may have mumbled my name under my breath. Shit, I was coming out in hot sweats, fizzing from the inside to the out. Kate. Kate. What a perfect, perfect name.

'I've seen you in the ice-cream shop,' she said.

'Yes,' I said.

'You always buy goody-goody gumdrops with a Flake and chocolate dip.'

'Yes.'

'I was just telling Kate all about the book I've been reading,' said Buckell in his loudest voice.

'I've seen you sit out on the beach, trailing sand through your fingers, watching the waves come in.'

'Yes.'

Her two ladies-in-waiting trailed over to our table, clutching their ciders in one hand and cigarettes in the other. I surreptitiously pushed the blackened pencil under the table and took two cigarettes out of my pocket. I handed one over the table towards her. She took it silently, without speaking, then raised it to her lips. My heart was singing in my chest. I felt I might explode around the pub in splinters of light. I had to see her again.

'Would you like to come and visit me at home?' I said.

'*What?*'

Shit. Now she was going to act all cool and casual.

'If I'm there, I mean. I probably won't be. I don't sit around waiting. I mean if you're passing. Which you won't be. But if you are . . . '

Shit. Where was that pencil? Floor. On the floor. Keep calm. Don't blow it now. I took a napkin out from under my pint and scribbled my address on it. I excused myself and headed for home.

Her name shone before it reached my ears. Light waves travel faster than sound waves; the lengths of the waves are shorter. Less resistant to the ether. Lightning, then . . . thunder. Kate Kate Kate. Her name was heat, light and sound. White liquid energy. Prisons of light and sound.

XIX

Kate

Work was just the same as bloody usual today. The flavours all just blur into one after a while. In your brain as well as in the container. My boss, Tess, doesn't believe in having a container of warm water to rinse the scoop off in, so bits of hokey-pokey get in the orange chocolate chip and bits of orange chocolate chip get in the Neapolitan. It's one of the hazards of the workplace, mixing flavours is. You never know exactly what it is that you're serving up. Still, the customers don't complain. Much.

We don't get that many people in during the week, just a few unemployed people and some old retired local residents. They all seem to own small fluffy dogs which they tie up outside the shop while they come in to stock up on Jeyes fluid and Kleenex and frozen veges. I like the way they move so slowly, although I don't doubt that arthritic limbs are more fun to watch than to be inside. I wonder what they do with their days. Do they just sit at home and stare at the walls, or are they active, some of them? I suppose you get all sorts really, like ice-cream flavours. I suppose they don't think they're old; you're only as old as you feel, they say. Perhaps they feel nineteen. But it'd only take one close-up look in the mirror and all your illusions'd be shattered like the glass itself. Perhaps you just wouldn't have any mirrors around the house. But then surely you'd catch a glimpse of yourself in a shop window every now and then and start to worry. I think about this sort of thing, you see, as I serve up your choc chip and your vanilla ice and your Fru-Ju. I watch you come into the shop, and I think about you. And if you fuck me off, then I think about you even more, and I try and imagine what it would be like to be you. I try to become you. I try to wake up in the morning in your bed, and go to the shower with you, and use your razor and fix your eggs and coffee with you and check the icebox with you and get your mail and listen to the radio and read the paper. That's what I do when I'm working. And you know what? The more of a wanker you are to me, the more I try and absorb you and bury you inside me. Some people say that the murderer absorbs the soul of the victim, but I say it's the other way round. I absorb all you bastards into me and I become you. I become all of you.

XX

Jim

In the kitchen, the phone was shrilling. The lights were out. There must have been a power cut. We live in a problem area: the neighbours are always complaining – steep electricity bills, and a lot of power failures. I picked up the receiver.

'Gary's sent me news.'

'Fuck off.'

'What?'

'Nothing. Sorry. It pays my rent to listen to you.'

'You live with your parents!'

'Pays my board.'

'What?'

'To write about you.'

'Are you getting smart?'

'No. Apologies.'

'You don't write about *me*, do you? Shit, that'd be a right bore.'

'You're telling me.'

'Thanks.'

'You said it. Anyway, do you want to hear the thing from Patricia or not?'

'It must be what she was writing on my window ledge. What'd it arrive by? Homing pigeon?'

'Are you all right? Have you been sleeping?'

'Yes. There's just a power cut and the whole house

is black. It's all right. I'm eating lots of carrots.'

'You sound funny. Is this Patricia thing getting to you?'

'No.'

'I was thinking. She couldn't have written it on your windowsill. It could never have got here so promptly. I think that may have been a figment of your rather overactive imagination, if you don't mind me saying so. Perhaps you unconsciously figure her as some sort of mother figure. It'll be all tied up with the castration complex. Perhaps you view her as what is abject and disgusting. Which would be odd, because she was terrifically ordered and well behaved. In a perverse and rather repressed kind of a way.'

'Cut the psychoanalysis and read the letter.'

'Are you listening?'

'My dearest Caroline,

I am here on the border, atop a high mountain range. To the east, the city shimmers on the far horizon against a sky of violent orange. To the west lies the circus, with all its promise of endless tomorrows. The altitude does not agree with me, and I find myself hacking up small round knobs of blood with mechanical regularity. The air is thin, and so cold it seems as if one is swallowing a series of sharp razor blades. I heard gunshots ringing out from the city harbour early this morning. A war memorial? I am tired and my bones are weary, but, oh, I have come so far. Caro, if I could begin to describe the brambles in the feet, the gorse clinging to the baby-blue cashmere sweater, the noise of the moreporks crying out from where they couch. I even snagged my foot in a rabbit trap whilst clambering through the last forest. Where was toenail now is bloody stump, but we shall not dwell on these wounds of war. I made the journey up the final cliff yesterday and set up my small tent in a convenient alcove. Oh, for a bed and breakfast now.

I shall be descending tomorrow, shall necessarily lose sight of the city in order to get closer to the circus. I look forward to meeting Rasputin. I shall be expecting to take a new lover. Yes, Caro, I am afraid that our Steven met a sticky end. You are shocked that we were lovers? Did you not pick up on that 'bumpy taxi ride through the city' in an earlier letter?

Yes, Steven met me all right, at the home. The fish that I had slipped down his shirt on our first meeting he had (oh! the miracles of alchemy!) taken to a jeweller, cast in bronze and set in the form of a brooch which I now wear pinned to my chest. Yes, Steven arrived as expected, fully kitted, only three hours late. We walked the distance to the bus stop. How can I say this? Brace yourself . . . A terrible accident befell the man.

Only one of us boarded the Greyhound. Yes, it's true. Steven the Raven was mown down by a truck carrying fireworks to a nearby Guy Fawkes celebration. A messy yet colourful finale to what was just blossoming into a fine love affair. Such is the way of love: temporary and messy. Better he finish in this manner than we grow bored and complacent together, as I am afraid myself and Bertie did as we aged. Better Steven be allocated to the cemetery of memory, where I may visit his grave with tulips whenever I fancy. So mention me to Rasputin, and I shall be by your side quite shortly.

P.G.'

Pause. Static on line.

'Glad to see she's lost that sickening note of self-righteousness and moral superiority. How shall we find her?'

'*God* knows where she is.'

My mother entered the room with a look of concern upon her face. She came over and took the phone off me, listened into the receiver and hung up. She took my hand and led me over to sit in a chair at the kitchen table.

'Who do you think you were talking to?'

I shrugged, hunched my shoulders and shook my head. My hair was getting longer; it fell over my face, slightly greasy, needing a wash. What should I use? Palmolive, Wella or just plain soap? These were the everyday choices: what to have for lunch, how to have my coffee. How should I live?

'There was nobody on the other end. You realise that, don't you? Red and I are very, very worried about you.'

Five-second pause. Pursing of lips.

'You've been *writing* again, haven't you?'

Shall I sleep seven hours a night, or eight? What clothes should I wear when I get up in the morning? On the end of one strand of hair hung a piece of white lint. I reached up and picked it off.

'A friend calling himself Buckell rang up here this afternoon. He said that you were behaving quite frantically at the pub. You're not coping with this death, are you?'

'What death?'

Three-second pause. Sigh of mild exasperation.

Should I take milk in my tea?

'Would you like to talk to somebody about it?'

Would too much coffee give me the jitters? Should I smoke? Do I drink too much alcohol?

'Who would you like to see?'

'Ringer.'

'Who on earth is Ringer?'

'He's just got out of prison.'

'I hardly think he sounds like the sort of person who

you should look to for help, love.'

'He didn't mean to do it. He was egged on.'

Am I killing brain cells with my alcoholic habits? Am I living as I should?

'Do what?'

'He loved his father, really.'

'I beg your pardon?'

'Sorry. I feel a bit sick.'

The table levitated for a brief moment before bucking out its two hind legs, giving a small whinny and settling its legs back down into the indentations on the linoleum.

'So who is this Ringer chap?'

'Nobody.'

'I'd actually like you to see somebody professional. Red and I would pay all the costs. Your mental health is a number-one concern.'

'Yes.'

'Why don't you go on up to your room, and we'll call you down for supper.'

I felt as if I were being wrapped in a thick sheet of cottonwool.

What can I say now?

Time passed.

XXI

Kate

It's irritating, isn't it, the way one person can get inside your brain and gnaw away like borer in a plank of wood. And it doesn't matter whether you hate them or you love them, they're just there. They fill in space, and you catch yourself talking to them mentally, just wondering what they'd think about this thing or that thing. And you don't need to have seen them that often either.

All right, I confess. He came into the shop the other day and did his staring act again. He never said anything neither, just kept on looking, like I was heaven-sent or something. Bet he wanks over me. I wouldn't be bloody surprised. And he did the stare-at-my-breasts trick again, so I leaned over the counter and stared down at where the bulge of his manhood *might* have been. Hardly hung like a racehorse. Puny little fella. He never asked for ice-cream neither just sort of pointed and drooled, and then headed towards the Caramel Chews. I gave him what he wanted, and he counted out the right change and everything. So he can't be as simple as he looks. I thought he might be a bit . . . you know . . . simple, but now I wonder if he has some sort of nervous disorder. He was certainly pretty twitchy. He'd probably just been working on a painting.

So I don't think much of him, you see, but from time to time I catch myself thinking about him as I'm getting dressed, or stepping into the shower, or fixing myself a coffee. And then I wonder what Maria would have thought of him. No doubt she would have been right bloody critical – she was like that, she was fucking picky about boys back then. Maybe she's different now, who knows? People change. Michelle thinks he's right bloody creepy and says she's never heard him say one word ever, and she reckons she's seen him at the Big Girl at least half a dozen times. She goes there more often than me. She likes her booze, does our Michelle. I reckon it'll be her downfall. I reckon it'll be the bloody end of her. She gets pissed three or four times a week, and lately it's been during the day. But like they say, you gotta look after number one. You've got to be all right for yourself or you're no bleeding use to anybody.

I can remember, you know, I can remember back when Dad was all right all the time. He used to come away on holiday with us and everything. I remember this one time when we all went away to Clipton, a real family thing, you know what I mean? We went away to Clipton when they were still building the dam upstream. The sign outside the hotel said, 'Right on the shores of beautiful Lake Pigeon', but there was no lake, there was only the river far off in the distance and the muddy front lawn of the grounds. The couple who owned the hotel were right bloody weird. 'Just new,' they said, 'just built. We're going to be right on the lakefront when they flood it. All those houses, all those roads down there, they're going underwater. Government's bought them all out.' I'm not one to get creeped out easily, but that made me feel kind of uneasy. It's hardly the lost city of Atlantis, but it's still pretty bizarre.

Dad enjoyed that holiday, though. He took his rods along with him and went trout fishing, relaxed. I'm not sure when it was that he actually began to get sick. I was still friends with Maria when he did, because I remember having to lie to her about why she couldn't come and stay over. I had to say, 'Sorry, my Mum says no, you can't come and stay', but the truth of it was that Dad'd locked himself away and was refusing to come out. He'd be all quiet and still in there, like the smooth surface of a lake, and then there'd be this huge volcanic eruption from the room. Even when he's not sick he's like that. The storm is always brewing and you just wait for it to erupt.

Damon was always the best at placating him. He was always the favourite and I was always the prodigal child. I suppose one of us had to be. There was no way in hell I was going to go work at the company with Dad for a boss. Not even if hell froze over. I doubt that I could've gone to work during one of Dad's crises, gathered all the workers into the smoko room and yelled, 'Your boss has been called away on urgent business. I'll be taking over for a week, everything'll carry on as usual.' If I'd been in there it would have been more like, 'Your boss has lost it. He's locked himself in his study at home, and he won't be coming out for at least a week. No, Herb, we have no idea what he does in there. Yes, my mother does leave meals outside the door, and when she goes back in an hour outside the door there *is* only an empty plate. You want to make a fucking big deal of it, do you?'

I don't wish to sound whiney or anything, but really, it becomes pretty damn hard to live out all Dad's lies for him. I've talked to Mum about it and everything, and she says that when she married him she didn't know that anything was wrong with him. There was only once, she said, when she went round to collect him to go to the movies and she called all round the house and there was no reply, and eventually she found him down in the cellar, playing puppets with his penis. She'd thought it was an isolated incident at the time.

Sometimes I wonder what it must be like to be inside somebody else's family, learning certain rules and not others. When I think about old Mr Creepy (which I don't very often), I try to imagine what his family are like. Perhaps he doesn't have a family at all. He *looks* like he hasn't had a shower in about a week, let alone a decent meal. He looks homeless. I think the measure of a family is how they behave on holiday together. I wonder if he goes on holidays with his family¿ I wonder if he goes to Clipton¿

The second time we went, Dad couldn't come with us, so Mum took the family stationwagon and off we went. The town now had a feeling of unbelievable newness to it, as if it were not made of real materials but cut out of cardboard and pasted on to the horizon. You could almost see it shining from the road on the other side of the river. It was night when we were driving into Clipton, and it had been raining, so the colours from the streetlights washed over everything.

We crossed over to the other side, the bridge arching high into space, the lamps at even intervals. Underneath is where the city used to be, the old Clipton, the one that was drowned. They say that not everybody wanted to sell up, and that some people were forced to move when the water began to creep up over their lawns and then up their doorsteps and then into their front living rooms.

The bridge is now concrete and steel, but underneath the water is the old wooden bridge, where the traffic used to cross. It's not so deep as all that, they say, this new river, this new lake. If you want to go diving, you can get down to the old bridge, and with scuba gear you can get down to the houses, which are deeper, and go through the empty rooms where the people of Clipton used to live. Beautiful Lake Pigeon.

We stayed in the same hotel, though the couple who owned it didn't remember us. We checked into a different room, one that was further away from the main office, from the prying eyes of Mr and Mrs Brannigan.

That first night I tried to sleep, but all I could think about was Dad, stuck away at home. We were trying to shock him by just up and leaving. Mum hadn't wanted him to starve, so she'd wrapped up all his meals, five of them, and left them outside the door, covered in gladwrap. Left them outside the door with labels on them, Monday to Friday. I wondered if he was all right back there at home. I felt so sorry for him, although I hated him as well. It grew worse and worse: you know how it is at night, when the shadows grow longer and the light recedes. It becomes that much harder to keep your perspective. I felt achy when I thought of him alone in the house. All night in my forehead things were shifting and blazing. I wanted to go diving.

For how long was I under? I was on the railing. It was late, I was looking west, with a hook where my mind might have been. Then I was diving from the new bridge, down past the old wooden one, and into the blackness. I must have been holding my breath, although I had my eyes open. In the darkness, visible were the curtains billowing out of the windows of the houses, and on one windowsill I could see an old, intricately painted porcelain vase, although there were no flowers in it. In the middle of the town was the old church, with the stained-glass window smashed in from the force of the water. Past that were the old carnival grounds. This was not my carnival, this was a toy. But it was a carnival all right. They hadn't moved it on when they drowned the town. Everything was as I had remembered it, only smaller, in miniature. Toy carousels with the horses frozen mid-gallop, toy house of mirrors, toy Ferris wheel. The toy quarters of the animals. Then I was surfacing up through everything, and I could breathe again.

In the morning my clothes were lying on the floor, wet, and I was in bed, naked. Damon was in the bed opposite mine, and I could hear Mum's snoring coming from the next room. I went in and woke her up, and suggested that perhaps we should give Dad a call, 'cause he has a phone in his study. She told me to piss off, so I went to the office and asked to borrow their phone. It rang and rang and rang. Ten rings with no reply. I couldn't bring myself to hang up, so I left the phone off the hook, just ringing, and ignored Mrs Brannigan yelling after me. Just what exactly was I thinking of, young lady, just leaving the phone off like that, people could have been trying to get through.

When I got back to our room, Mum and Damon were up preparing coffee and eggs and oranges for breakfast. I said I didn't feel hungry, and that I was going for a walk. I was out on the road, and then it was happening again, they were behind me, grabbing my hair, and holding my arms and then they were on top of me and forcing me down. There were two or three or four of them. And then we were amongst some straw, like in a barn, or in the quarters of one of the animals, and then two of them, or one of them, had my arms, and Maria's head was sliding around the edge of the building.

I am back there again, my mind on loop tape. I close my eyes and I am falling into darkness, back into the carnival, inside a black hole, over the edge of the cliff, over the railing of the bridge. I dream I am somebody else, slipping sideways out of my body, like fainting, the wind rushing past my ears, I am falling faster than the speed of light. I close my eyes and I am falling into nothingness.

When I wake up, I have another name. I am older than myself.

XXII

KATHERINE

I woke in the morning, rolled over and grasped his body, warm as it always is. I held on to his back for two or three minutes, to warm myself, then rose from the bed and went into the kitchen to make us both a cup of coffee. Sometimes, when I think about the feminist movement (which James likens to a bowel movement), I feel bad about this, but most of the time I don't think. Most of the time I act out of habit, and because he's an artist with a dreadful temper. So I feel it is necessary to tiptoe around him. And on weekends he cooks me omelette on toast, and brings me a glass of milk fresh from delivery. Except on Sundays, when the milkman doesn't call.

He's been happy lately, having just received a grant for three thousand dollars from the Arts Council. He's happy not to have to depend on me for financial support like he used to. It's not good for a man to feel too dependent on a woman. Especially not a painter. He needs his own space, which is why I work at the hospital. Oh, and to earn money for myself of course. Theresa, my boss at the clinic, keeps trying to tell me that I have a dependency problem, but it's not like that at all. It's just that I really care for people, and like to see them happy. I like to make James happy; that's why I bring him his coffee in the morning. One milk, two sugars, though sugar makes him manic. When he gets like that, I just go off to the gym and leave him at it. Once, when I came back, there was paint all over the dining room carpet, James was naked, and had the paintbrush strapped to his penis. He had a frightful erection. I couldn't believe it. The dog had run from the room in terror. I just stood there, not knowing what to say. Eventually I had to say, Look, James, this is just not on. He looked at me then, but didn't see me. His eyes were glazed and distant, as if he were gazing somewhere else. I detected a faint feral gleam. Eventually he came down and crashed. Lay around staring at blank walls for three weeks after that. Neil, that's Theresa's husband, came round and stuck him on Lithium, but he's not sick, really. Not like the rehab patients. Some of those are really loop-the-loop. They come down off whatever addiction has been holding them in the air, and they fall completely to pieces. My favourite one, Griselda, has been a junkie since she was thirteen, and tells me she is now living in the post-apocalyptic age. She thinks she's on an island called Malata, the only island to have survived the explosion. I hear all about the interesting landscapes created by a nuclear winter. In some ways she reminds me of James, only she's not so highly strung. They both inhabit fantasy worlds, only James receives government funding for his. Griselda just raves. You should hear her. On and on and on. Quite often we have to tape her mouth shut or lock her in the 'time-out' room till she calms down. Next door to her is Tommy, the reforming alcoholic who suffers from echolalia, and a chap with agoraphobia. I don't believe in medicine. The mind will find its own cure. Will-power over insanity.

All human beings need to be decently occupied. Occupational therapy isn't all cane baskets and fluffy kittens, you know. We help each individual to find their own little niche. It's very important for a person to feel of use in this society of ours. Very important. James says it's his duty to society to paint, and that he does his best to serve mankind. He's quite good. Like I said, he got that grant, and he's exhibiting at a café next week. As for me, well, I get my kicks from helping others, I really do. Otherwise I wouldn't be in my line of work. I'd be a corporate mogul, or a gardener or something.

So I woke in the morning, and went downstairs to get James his coffee, and when I came back to bed he was up and into the shower, so I just left the coffee on the dresser next to his bed and got dressed. I'd had my shower the night before, you see. So I got into my black work cullottes and my purple shirt. I like to wear purple to the clinic, it brightens the place up a bit. When I was dressed, I poked my head around the bathroom door to shout goodbye to James. Through the perspex shower door I could see the outline of his body, the hairs matting together with the water. I remember when we used to shower together: we're both too busy now. And besides, the shower's really too small for that: one person always ends up getting cold. And in winter it's so easy to catch the flu. James has been as sick as a dog. So I yelled goodbye, and then I headed out for work. Luckily the hospital's within walking distance, because we can't afford a car.

When I arrived at work, Theresa and Neil were having a bite to eat in the staffroom. It's so lovely the way some couples can work together and yet still maintain a good relationship. I really admire that. Still. You can't really beat what James and I have together.

XXIII

James

When the first ray of light fell across the sash of the window, I awoke. I was not waking to grey light, as I had been for the past few weeks. This light was white, and fell in a thin sliver, like the shaft of a sword. I reached over to grasp Katherine, but she wasn't there, which was a pity, because I like her in the mornings, when she's slightly cold. It's because she's so thin that she gets cold like that. I lay and stared at the light for a while, then eased myself up to head for the shower. It's getting dirty in there, I noticed, spots of black fungus decorating the ceiling. Something for me to do in between canvases, clean out the shower.

I'm working on a new piece. It's called 'Still Life With Bear At Circus' and is composed of two roses, a pear, a salmon, two sea tulips and a grizzly. I had a bit of trouble with the grizzly. In particular, his right paw looked clumsy. You know how it's hard to paint human hands (they always end up looking like sausages)? Well it's even harder to paint bears' paws. This paw ended up looking like a fish, so I turned it into a salmon and pretended he'd had a fresh catch. Don't know if there's much public demand for bears with salmon, but you can't argue with divine inspiration. Or divine desperation. Then there was the problem with his ears. They got bigger and whiter, till they turned into wings. So he became a bear with the power of flight. Poor bastard. I was scared the whole thing was going to end up looking like one of those tacky posters you can buy in new-age shops, with the cat-woman's face in the foreground and a wispy bird figure tucked in behind. But I managed to save the picture. That's what I'm going to work on today. Today I'll perfect the pear. I think it needs a blemish. Who were those painters who used to have imps peeping out from under the skirts of the angels? Or am I thinking of flaws woven into Persian carpets? Never did manage to pass an art history paper. Still, all that's for the birds really; for a true artist, instinct alone is enough.

Katherine understands this. She's not a bad bit, really. I love her, though I don't know what that means. We're not married or anything, we're just partners, or lovers, or living together. Depends on who we're talking to. One thing she's damn well *not* is my other half. God how I hate that expression. It makes us sound so . . . well, so . . . so *dependent*. And incomplete. Love . . . I love her because she never moans about my painting, and she understands my moods. When I was younger I could bash myself over the head with an iron pipe during a manic fit and still not feel anything. Then two days later I'd be frozen solid with despair. It takes a special kind of a woman to put up with that kind of thing. I was one big ego back then – insatiable, hungry and furious. Awake with a vengeance.

Katherine understood this, said she's seen it at the hospital. It was lucky she worked there *that* night actually, 'cause it meant she could ring up her boss, and he could come round with some lollies to calm me down. That was the night I nearly set the dog on fire, my painting on fire, the oven on fire, the curtains on fire. Nearly burnt the whole fucking house down. She'd come home from work, you see, and caught me, mid-flight, paintbrush strapped to my cock, and paint all over my body. How embarrassing. I was doing a self-portrait called 'Artist and His Mania', and needed to get my whole body into it, so as to get the full effect. When she saw me like that she went to the gym, I think, came back, and I was rubbing myself all over the canvas. Never have I seen such horror. By the time her boss came round I had a shirt on at least, but the dining room and I were still pretty filthy, and there was a trail of paint leading from my studio down the hall to the painting. I'd had to go to the dining room to paint it, you see. Don't ask me why, I just *had* to. He gave me something to calm me down right away, then prescribed Lithium just like that. It's good too. Oh, there's a bit of constipation and nausea, but I don't get high like I used to, not so high that I can't control it, high like out on the edge, tightrope-walking, not knowing when you're going to fall. And things have improved between Katherine and me. We're going out more, to clubs and that, having dinner with friends, and entertaining guests and visitors, and I'm not draining her energy like I used to. I love her, really. She means the world to me, even though I might not always show it.

I'm like my Dad in that way. He was a farming bloke, and only ever grunted at Mum. But I'm learning. I even bought her some lilies the other week. Should have seen her face. Lit up like a bloody Christmas tree. Never seen her so happy. It's amazing how a woman blossoms beneath the love of a good man.

XXIV

Katherine

Griselda was at her oddest today. I tell you, I've spent so much time around the clinically disturbed lately, I've forgotten what normal is. Not, of course, that I like to put people in little boxes, sane and insane, but it does help you to keep your own grip on reality when you have some sort of reference point of normalcy.

Griselda's big thing is fimo. Last week she made a cute wee fish with purple and green stripes. Then she made a crocodile, which ate the fish. I wonder what that could mean? Perhaps she feels that she is being devoured by her 'illness'. I don't like to call it that, not really. It's not an illness; only something inside, some enemy which takes hold and grows. By the time it gets a few roots down, it's so hard to yank out.

Griselda is being overtaken by a giant venus flytrap, just like in that movie, the one with the dentist and the blonde. *Little Shop Of Horrors*. That's it. That plant is inside her. Some days you'd swear she's winning, and she'll be released within the week, then on other days she seems even worse than old Tommy with his echolalia. Some days it's as if she speaks words without even knowing what she's saying. Some days I am sure I am listening to the song of the venus flytrap.

XXV

JAMES

Even though my blemish looks like shit and my salmon's the colour of menstrual blood, I still think it's a blessing that I never went to art school. 'Cause if I had, I probably would have ended up like one of those wankers who knows the flavour of every wine on a wine list. 'Refined in the nose, wouldn't you say? Fruity on the palate, exploding in a cascade of flowers in the throat.' Something like that anyway. Those sort of people who don't pronouce the 't' in Camembert. I always make sure I emphasise the 't' when I say that word, just so as to show I'm not a wanker. I like to make them think I'm an idiot: gets them on the back foot. Then you can come out with some sophisticated French, like '*Quell heur es teil*', and they know that they're dealing with an artist of force. Those bastards who know their wine and cheese. I know the bloody sort. *This world artists*, I call them, 'cause they're only interested in the attention they get and who's speaking their name. Hate that sort of shit. Tell you what, you'd never catch me doing no interview for no snotty magazine. Never catch me being called a 'culture vulture'. The only vultures'll be in my paintings. Call me an anti-social bastard if you will. I just want to paint the best pictures possible. And sell them of course.

In some ways it's lucky I go out with Katherine. She's so stable. She really is a pillar of absolute stability. I think it comes from having grown up in a family like that. Oh, don't get me wrong. I don't look down on them or anything. It's just that . . . well . . . they do say that the children of alcoholic fathers tend to be either alcoholics themselves or else overly caring towards other people. She's very caring, Katherine. But you know, sometimes, just sometimes I get a little bit tired of playing the fucked-up painter to her oh-so-responsible therapist. Sometimes I wonder if it's not something sick inside of her that makes her want to mother me. I mean, what is it about her that attracts her to the tired and the wounded and the sick? Of course, nobody would go so far as to mention the word martyr . . . Sometimes I feel guilty about how much she gives to me. But I really don't think she'd have it any other way. Everybody says how lovely she is. That's the adjective they use, lovely. Lovely Katherine. Isn't she lovely? Isn't it lovely the way that Katherine . . . (takes care of others / bakes scones / is so understanding / always has time to listen . . .) ad infinitum, ad fucking nauseam. Enough to make you . . . happy for her. I hate to think how they talk about me. Isn't it *awful* the way James . . . (drains Katherine of all her energy / hasn't sold a painting in two years / never has time for anyone else . . .). Pack of gossiping liars, the lot of them.

XXVI

Katherine

I really wanted to visit my friend Francoise on the way home, so I thought, Well, what the heck, Katherine, why not treat yourself? You deserve some time to yourself. So I dropped by the supermarket to get a few things for James's dinner, then I walked round to her place. She's a dance teacher. Great body. Not an ounce of flab on her. Toned and taut. Not that she flaunts it. She *has* to wear leotards outside dance class; she doesn't own anything else. Oh no, I tell a lie. She has a pair of those bubblegum jeans that were in during the '80s. Still, she'd look good in a potato sack, Francoise would, so it doesn't really matter that no one's worn jeans like that for ten years. She sets her own fashion standards, does our Franny. Always has, always will. Anyway, I got to her place and she had a pupil she was tutoring so I had to wait in the front room for five minutes or so, but I didn't mind.

I know I'm being a bit bitchy about Franny. But it's only the sort of criticism you make about the people you love the most. You know, the old familiarity breeds contempt thing. Not that she is that familiar; I haven't had the time to visit her in the last month. But I know what she'll say when she sees me. She'll say, 'Oh how *lovely*, Katherine has come to visit.' That's what I am to her. Lovely. I am lovely. Everybody says it. So giving, so selfless. Sometimes I wonder what the border between selfless and self-effacing is.

I've had a real shit of a day. Negative vibes, you know? I really can get as titchy as the next woman. It's just that nobody sees it. Some people are like hurricanes: they're up and they're down, but they're always in the grips of some mood or another. That's James. And then we have Francoise, who vents her stress through physical movement, through exercise. She's like an animal in that way – a very bodily person. I'm more spiritual. Crystal round the neck. That's what I try and focus on when I feel tension building up inside. James and I have one of those prisms with water in over the kitchen sink, too. One of those ones with water in that create those wonderful rainbow colours. I always feel a bit sad when I look at that water, because it seems so trapped. I mean, it was a river once, wasn't it? And now it's stuck inside a bit of glass. Perhaps it was just ordinary tap water, although the label on the bottle does say that it was taken fresh from Pupu Springs. But you know these new-agers, they lie through their teeth. Anything to make a buck.

But there I was, waiting in the front room, when the little ponytailed pupil trotted out past me and in waltzed Francoise.

'Oh darling,' she cooed, and I was embraced in a swoon of Obsession (her perfume). She patted my bottom.

'Gosh, don't *you* look healthy. James's been cooking you up a few steak dinners, I suppose. He does do a wonderful pepper sauce.'

'Ummm, no. Actually, I do most of the cooking these days. James is too busy working on "Still Life With Bear At Circus".'

'Still *what?*'

'Still Life With Bear At Circus. He says it's to be his seminal work.'

'Oh, I don't know if I like the sound of that. Katherine, there haven't been any more . . . accidents, have there?'

'You make him sound like a dog that wets the carpet. No. No accidents.'

'He's still on . . . medication?'

'Yes. Let's not talk about him. I've come to see you. Let's talk about you. What've you been up to?'

'Oh, you know, just plodding along, giving my lessons to reluctant thirteen-year-olds. Teaching the girls how to smile, smile, smile, dealing with stage mums, all that sort of rubbish. And you? How's work? Any new patients?'

'Yes, one. Griselda. Just the normal sufferance of manic delusions.'

'Goodness, how exciting.'

'Perhaps from the outside only.'

'And what does that mean?'

'Nothing, nothing, just musing to myself. You don't want to go for a coffee, do you?'

'Look, Katherine, I'd love to, only I've got another lesson to give in a quarter of an hour. Can we meet for lunch next week? We've got some catching up to do, haven't we?'

So we left it at that. A lunch date next week. We get on so well, we're as close as blood sisters. Of course James hates her. He's jealous, I think. Although he pretends that he likes me to have other friends, if I get too close to anybody he always starts complaining that I don't spend enough time with him. He says that Francoise looks like she's had silicone implants, which isn't a very nice thing to say – and anyway, I know it's not true, because I've flown on a plane with Francoise and her breasts didn't burst. Also, I've known her for an awfully long time and her breasts have always been double D. Still, James can see right through people's appearances. That's one of his best qualities. The ability to see right through people's lies and pretences and into their hearts. Sometimes, you'd swear he was psychic.

On the way back to the flat, something about my conversation with Francoise was beginning to bother me. For three blocks I couldn't think what it was. Then I remembered. James's pepper sauce. We've never had her around for dinner. A few beers, yes, but never dinner.

XXVII

James

Let's get to work on the bear's nose. Looks a bit snotty at the moment. Better fix that up. Shit, I really can't be fucked. I've never been a great one for details. Perfectionism's not really my thing. If a thing's worth doing, it's worth doing well, they say, and I suppose there's some truth in that. I just don't have the patience for going back and doing the necessary yet totally boring *tidying up*. I suppose I'll learn, eventually, the hard way. But for now it's dinner time. God, wish Katherine'd hurry back with the steak. Suppose she's off galavanting all over the bloody neighbourhood, talking to . . . never mind. I suppose I should get my shit together and start the pepper sauce, her favourite. A lot of women enjoy that sauce. Actually, I hate to say it, but I do think it expresses something of my personality. Sort of fiery and saucy and . . .

Here she is! Hello, darling, you got the steak? Fantastic. Don't suppose you thought to pick up any . . . capers? No. Garlic? No. Any . . . peppercorns, by chance? Ah, well. Necessity is the mother of all invention.

Did you know that some friends of ours, the Gavins, have their baby's umbilical cord on the shelf with the spices? They put it in the cooking. We went there for a pot-luck dinner once, and everybody'd been commenting on the curry and what was that delicious unidentifiable flavour, and Katherine had little Jacob on her knee and was reading to him from a story book, and then somebody spotted this white shrivelled thing on the shelf next to the cumin. 'What on earth is that piece of string doing up on the spice shelf?' inquired a puzzled Francoise who had also been present at this particular soirée. Gabriella Gavin walked proudly to the shelf. 'This? This was the cord that bonded Jacob and I. We like to cook with it. A sort of new-age communion ceremony, we like to think.'

Poor little Jacob flew from Katherine's lap and landed in a sunken heap on the floor, never to be touched by another guest. Many of those seated clasped hands to their mouths in fear of the return of the digested. Katherine ran from the room with a look of horror on her face. It was only Francoise who handled it calmly. Scarcely a ripple of consternation ran across the calm millpond of her features. She clapped her hands briskly, twice, and said, 'Gosh, how exciting. I do love to try new and exotic things. Did you know that I have eaten crocodile and snake and tiger penis. Yes, tiger penis. And what's more, Siberian tiger penis. I know, frightfully naughty of me, the poor large things being nearly extinct and all. But still, it was well dead and gone when it landed on my plate. My not eating it would hardly have brought it back to life now, would it?' She stared at me intently from across the table, and I felt the press of her high heel against my boot. She's well endowed, Francoise is, if you know what I mean.

Although we have received several invitations to dine with the Gavins since then, we have been forced to politely refuse. I am afraid that peppercorns are as exotic as I choose to get. Still, like I said, the girls enjoy them, and that's the main thing. I like to give pleasure.

Now. If I do this sauce right, she won't even notice the pepper is powder. Perhaps if I sort of shove it together in clumps she might be fooled. And then again . . .

XXVIII

Katherine

Sometimes I wonder what kind of idiot he thinks I am. The steak was disgusting. Still, I suppose he *tried*, and that's all you can ask from a man. Can't ask much more from him in the bedroom these days, either. He's so distracted and inattentive. His mind is somewhere else. No doubt engrossed in 'Still Life With Bear At Circus'.

Speaking of minds that are somewhere else. Griselda. Today, when I went into her room with her breakfast (eggs and orange juice on a tray), she turned from where she was sitting looking out through the windowpane and said, 'They were wrong about the cockroaches.' Well what can you say? I nodded sympathetically.

'I'm sure they're wrong about a lot of things, Griselda.'

'Everything's bleached.'

'Yes. They do tend to use a lot of Janola on the floors.'

'They have bleached out the landscape with a cleaner's mop.'

'Yes.'

Nervous silence.

'And I have been colder and colder'

'Shall I get you another blanket?'

'Malata. I sailed across the endless glass sheet, the amniotic salinity of the ocean. You understand, the ocean is part fact, part fiction.'

'Mm-hm.'

'Sometimes I think I am the only surviver of this apocalypse, and then I hear, on the radio, and on the television, that there are others. When I listen. Through the white crackle of sound waves. Through reading the washroom walls. Through the whispers and the huddled silences.'

None of this talk was new to me. It was the sort of stuff she spouted all the time. And none of the stories cohered. Television after the holocaust? I think not. Still, she interests me more than the other patients. I sort of wish that she was my sister, so that I could take her home and sort her out once and for all. I'm sure it's just an attention thing, really.

XXIX

JAMES

Of course, she's not really a patch on Katherine, but she's not unattractive, Francoise. I know what you're thinking. You think I want to get into her pants, don't you? Well fuck you. I'm happy with what I've got. I'm not into melons for breasts. I prefer small round apples. Sorry about the fruit analogy. I don't really think of women as made for my consumption.

I only cooked her my special pepper steak that once. It was after the dinner at the Gavins. She called in to see Katherine, only Katherine was still at the clinic. So I had to entertain her. I was pretty pissed off actually, because I was in the middle of a painting entitled 'Black Digits on White Paper'. That was what I worked on before 'Still Life With Bear At Circus'. It was a tremendous success. Received much praise when I exhibited it at the local city gallery along with a few of my other small masterpieces. Anyway, I was just working on the number '3' when Francoise came into my studio looking for Katherine. She was hot and sweaty and smelt a little gamey. Not that I'm averse to a little sweat and body fluid. I tried to get rid of her, making delicate hints like, 'She's not here', and 'I need to get back to my painting', but she just stood there and watched me work, and I couldn't concentrate, couldn't lose myself, so I had to ask her for dinner.

If you want to know the truth, I felt sorry for her. I mean, she must get starving hungry, teaching those dance classes all day. You have to keep your iron count up when you do that sort of physical stuff. Must be something soft and pliable in me, but I just can't stand to see a woman go hungry. Anyway, we both knew that Katherine would be coming home at any minute. I cooked for three: it was just that she didn't come home at the time she usually does, so we ended up splitting her bit of steak and pepper sauce in half and sharing it between us. As you do.

I don't even like her much. I don't like her at all. I don't like anything about her. I don't like the way her hair hangs down all wet over the back of her neck, and I don't like the way she sits and laughs and moves her head. I don't even think about her. I don't even think about her when I get out of bed, or when I'm in the shower, or when I'm walking down the street in the evening and the street lamps are just beginning to flicker alight.

XXX

KATHERINE

Powdered pepper on the steak. I *still* can't believe it. You know what that is, don't you? That's an indication that our relationship's taking A turn for the worse. *Near* pepper sauce, indeed. The next thing you know we'll be having near champagne. Actually, Marque Vue has always been a secret little favourite. We don't buy alcohol often, as James considers he has a way with home brew. I can't stand the stuff myself, although Francoise, on the occasions on which she has tried it, has appeared very fond of its flavour. 'So wonderfully *yeasty*,' she'll say, and rub James's leg with her foot. Don't think I haven't noticed. I know exactly how they flirt. Sometimes I pretend I've noticed, and sometimes I don't. Sometimes I get the feeling James just thinks of me as some sort of slave, here at his beck and call twenty hours a day, seven days a week.

XXXI

James

She came around again tonight. Looking for Katherine again. Of course. She looked, she looked ... indescribable. Her hair hung down around her shoulders ... Oh God, Oh God. She's so fucking beautiful, who am I kidding. I feel as if I've known her for ever. When she looks at me ... I feel faint.

I kept painting and tried to ignore her, but she came up behind me, and pressed her shoulder against mine and I could feel the warmth of her body against mine. Our arms exchanged electrons. The strokes of my paintbrush became more and more frantic as I tried to ignore her presence. Oh God, my hands had a will of their own. Suddenly, without my direction, my right hand shot out and embraced her around the waist. Suddenly my lips shot out from my face and landed upon her lips. Suddenly, my tongue ... well, anyway.

Oh God, Katherine, I'm so, so sorry. We fell. We fell together, the two of us, to the floor, in a haze of tempestuous passion. She was every woman, every face, every body. She was my temptress, my femme fatale, my demon and my angel, my dark lady encased in glowing white. This dance is so brutal. She teaches me the waltz, the foxtrot, the highland fling, the can-can. God, compared to this Katherine is ... a side shuffle at a high school dance. Katherine, I'm so sorry.

How can I go on lying to you? I'm not in love with you. Or with her. Love? The word has no meaning. The experience that Francoise and I have together is beyond all language and beyond all expression. It is heaven and hell and limbo. It is the softest karate kick and the strongest spider web. Shit. I sound like I'm preaching from the pulpit.

XXXII

Katherine

Animals, absolute animals. I've never *seen* such a display of carnality. In his studio. In his *studio*. God knows how long they've been carrying on like this. Don't think I'm going to put up with it. I told him he had precisely twenty-four hours to pack his bags and piss off. And *she*, well, she just stood there clutching 'Still Life With Bear At Circus' in front of her genitalia and trying to pretend like she'd just been nude modelling for him. I told her that both our lunch date and our friendship were terminated. I mean, I knew she'd enjoyed the odd *flirtation* with him, but an actual affair? Too much, too much, too much.

XXXIII

JAMES

I don't care, I don't give a stuff, two hoots, a damn carbuncle. I have what I want. Who cares if I have to live out on the street. Of course I won't have to live on the street. I have friends. I'll go and stay with Marty, or even . . . no don't be stupid. Francoise wouldn't want me. Living together would ruin everything. Better to play it cool and calm, just casual screwing. Marty'll let me in. And I'm sure he won't find it objectionable that I set up my studio in his garage. He'll probably let me set up 'Bear' in his living room. Speaking of bear, it's coming along really well. I should be finished by the end of the month. It's a fucking inconvenience having to move out so suddenly, but . . . you can only go on living a lie for so long. This is my last night in Katherine's flat – on the sofa, of course. But tomorrow, sweet tomorrow, I'll go around and settle myself in at Marty's and then I'll go straight to the florists, and then I'll go around to Francoise's place and we'll do it all over the house. She makes me feel like a teenager again, all hot and flustered and excited, with my heart racing and my palms secreting.

Katherine and I weren't really working out anyway. We were only biding time till we broke up. She's a sweet girl: she'll forgive us both. In time.

XXXIV

KATHERINE

Fuck him, fuck him, fuck him, fuck. Do you know what it's like to hate someone so much that you feel nauseous when you think about them? Well I hate him more than that. Fuck her, fuck her, fuck her, fuck. You know, I have this little problem. I can't decide which one of them I hate more. I hate *her* for trading in a friendship for a fuck, and I hate *him* for trading in a relationship for a fuck. I mean, was I not worth something?

I can't believe that I have been *such* an idiot. I should have severed the flirtation in its first delicate stages rather than letting it come to this. Forget nipping it in the bud. I should have yanked the whole plant from the soil, screaming roots and all. It's just that you don't think it, do you? You don't think that your best mate would screw your man. And now it's happened. All I can say is, I'm glad I've got my job. Where would you be without your income and your independence? Sure it might not be the best job in the world, but still, at the end of the day, it brings in a wage, doesn't it? That's more than you could ever say about 'Still Life With Bear At Circus'.

Whoever would have thought that *Griselda* would have become a point of stability for *me*?

XXXV

JAMES

Endless sex, endless sex, endless sex. She's the best fuck in the world, I swear to God. And everything with Marty is great. I'm sleeping in the living room, right next to 'Still Life With Bear At Circus'. Actually, it's beginning to give me quite severe nightmares about being chased by giant bears with salmon sprouting from their paws. And then the bears turn into thousands of Katherines and they pursue me down thousands of endless corridors. And then I wake up on the sofa with my own wing-eared bear gawking down at me. Or, more recently, I wake up in behind Francoise. The old morning broomhandle-in-the-back. Wink, wink, nudge, nudge, say no more.

XXXVI

Katherine

They say that revenge is a woman's art. They say that revenge is bittersweet. Fuck them. Why should I lower myself to petty comebacks and the spreading of vicious rumours? I shall remain above and aloof. He'll come crawling back. Like a dog returning to its true master. When he gets sick of her, when he's used up all his lust (and believe me, there's no question of anything more than that), when he's finally tired of bonking her senseless, that is when he'll come crying back to me. There he'll be snivelling on my doorstep, saying he's got nowhere to live, saying he does, always has and always will love me, that he wants only me. And of course I shall not lose my cool. I shall remain calm and orderly. I shall smile and extend my arms towards him in a gesture of benevolence and unlimited love. And then I'll jerk back suddenly, as if I were a puppet controlled by strings, and I'll say, 'Gosh, am I mistaken, or did we once have a relationship together?' And he'll say, 'Yes, yes, darling, it's me, your little James, come home to you, his one true love.' And I'll say, 'God, but you look disgusting. I mean you used to look disgusting before, but now you look ten times worse. Is that lice I see in your hair? Is that a *beard* on your chin? Is that *vomit* trapped within the bristles of your beard? No. No, I refuse to believe it. James would never let himself go like that. You must be an impostor. You can't be my James.' He'll start to cry and beg, and I'll shut the door. Not a slam, mind, just softly and with a slight note of condescension, as you would on any unwanted visitor.

I shall not resort to petty acts of violence.

XXXVII

JAMES

When I catch the bastard. When I catch that fucker, I'll rip his balls from his groin, then I'll yank out his heart from his chest and eat it. Still beating, I'll eat it arteries and all. When I catch that motherfucker, I'll strip him naked and tie him to a lamp-post in the middle of the town and leave him there till the morning, when everybody can laugh at his shrivelled and frozen dick. When I catch that arsehole . . .

We'd been screwing in the afternoon, hadn't we? Francoise had telephoned little Doris, or Norris, or Loris, and cancelled that afternoon's tap/ballet/modern dance lesson. It was all over the house shagging, you know what I mean? Kitchen, hallway, bathroom, bedroom, back yard, etc, etc. I'd left her tired and love-weary out in the garden shed, and gone back to Marty's to get some dinner ready for when he got home from work.

I could see the smouldering from the street corner. Talk about KKK, burning crosses and all that. I wasn't that worried at first, presuming it would just be Marty home early, having a burn-up in the back yard. Then, as I got closer, I saw that the smoke wasn't coming from the back yard at all but appeared to be rising up from the very pavement itself. What a bloody mess! In front of the house, I thought, what a stupid place for an incineration. The leaves and sticks and ash would be bound to blow all down the street, set the neighbour's roses on fire and create general havoc. Then I got even closer and I noticed a remarkable *absence* of leaves and sticks and branches. The thing looked like a square chunk of wood. And oh shit, is that the winged ear of a bear that I see emitting a thin yet steady stream of smoke? Please, no. Oh please, no. I feel violated, I feel sick. Days and nights and nights and days of work, on fire, on fire. Reaching the heavens maybe, but in entirely the wrong way. Oh, who would do this? Who would do this to me?

XXXVIII

Katherine

Oh, you can't prove anything. Did you see me do it? I never stole in through the lounge window. And I never dragged the painting down the hallway and out through the main door. I never poured kerosene on the canvas and laughed in pure delight as 'Still Life With Bear At Circus' dissolved into flame. I'm not the vengeful type. In fact, I have three witnesses to verify that I was at the clinic at the time of the fire: Theresa, Neil and Griselda. So no one can prove anything. For all anyone knows it may have been the neighbours or Marty or the Klu Klux Klan. Go on. Try and say I'm guilty. I don't care, don't care, don't care.

So life goes on as before. The hospital, the friends to visit, the gym and the long walks along the beach. The empty bed. The empty chair where he used to sit and drink his cheap home brew. The empty space on the lounge wall where 'Bear' used to lean. No. No, no, no. I won't give in to it. I won't succumb to self-pity and despair. I am strong and good.

Actually, I have posted a few such messages in opportune sites about the flat. Open the medicine cabinet and you'll find a white slip of paper reading, 'I approve of Katherine, the universe is love.' Open up the fridge, check the icebox and you'll find, 'I am a happy and positive person.' Open the cupboard under the sink and you'll read, 'I am content with my own company.' Also, I have read in all the magazines that a period of mourning is healthy after a break-up. Not that I am in mourning. I don't even miss him. Not one little iota. All the magazines say the same thing: 'Treat yourself. Take a hot bath every evening, and use bath salts to give your body a delicious and natural fragrance. Soon all the men at your workplace will be commenting on the subtle yet vivacious odour which exudes from your very pores.' 'Burn all your photographs. Except the biggest one. Tape the biggest photo to the wall behind your bed. Buy some darts. Throw the darts. Invent your own bull's eye.' The magazines say, 'Make some new and exciting friends. Soon you'll forget all about the past, and concentrate on creating a positive future for yourself.'

But they don't tell me how to deal with this gaping fucking hole. This gaping black hole that sits in the middle of my chest when I wake up, when I shower, when I go to work, when I eat and when I sleep.

XXXIX

James

They say that something good will always come of something evil. And now I believe them. Something fantastic has sprung from this violent act of destruction which has been performed. Francoise has taken such pity on me that she has offered me the use of her basement as a studio. Of course, you know what I am thinking. My see-through skin lets me down again. It's just one small step from daytime residence to full day-in, day-out living. All it will take is one little, 'I'm so tired, and I'll want to paint first thing in the morning. You know how an artist gets all inspired when he first wakes up.' And her reply: 'Why, James, wouldn't it just be easier if you moved in completely? I mean, you already stay here three nights a week, and all your painting gear is here. How much more convenient for you to live with me.'

I want to settle down with her. I want to impregnate her. I want to grow old by her side. I've never felt that way about anyone.

XL

Katherine

Life goes on. Time marches on. Onward Christian soldiers. Except that last one's a bit wrong 'cause I'm an atheist.

I have taken up hockey. This is a good communal sport, and a fantastic way to meet new people. I have had a couple of one-night stands. Warren from the gym, and a guy that I picked up at the beach. His name was . . . oh, I forget. Anyway. I didn't really mean that about the black hole. I was just having a bad day. You know how it is. Anyway, better go to work.

XLI

JAMES

I could lie to you and tell you that we hate each other already. I could lie to you and say that the sex has become boring. I could lie to you and tell you I haven't been able to paint. Then you would think that justice has been served. What can I say? Sorry. Everything's great, fucking great. I've started a new work entitled, 'Black Strap Scone Dough Voodoo'. We screw most of the morning, and in the afternoon Francoise gives dancing lessons and I work on 'Scone'. Heaven is a place on earth.

You know what? I found out that it was her. Marty saw her running down the street with a kerosene can in her hand. And you know what? That bitch never got away with nothing. She thinks she can get revenge on me? She hasn't got a clue what fire is. I'll show her what fucking fire is.

XLII

Katherine

Everything was usual when I arrived at work. I did my usual check on the patients. Tommy was his usual self. Echolalia. What a pain.

'How are you this morning, Tommy?'

'Tommy?'

'Did you sleep well?'

'Sleep well?'

'Are you going for a walk today?'

'Walk today?'

Griselda was her usual self. Raving raving raving, on and on and on. I couldn't handle her today, I wasn't in the mood. Oh, I know I'm paid to handle it, but I'm only human.

I was down in the main reception, helping Theresa and Neil out with some filing. The smoke came softly at first, just creeping down the stairs like a shadow, and then in great giant billows, big folds of smoke, like sheets taken from a bed and hung out to dry in the wind. We were running towards the main doors and then I was choking and coughing and then everything was black.

XLIII

JAMES

So it doesn't pay to mess with me, all right? 'Cause if you hit me one, I'll just hit you back two, and if you kick me four, I'll just kick you back eight.

XLIV

KATHERINE

I never came to myself. Everything was black, then everything was white and falling away, and I knew all about the holocaust because Griselda was right beside me, and showing me all around the island, and I was listening to the radio and the television and trying to say what I couldn't and nothing was ever communicated and nothing was ever said. I never came to myself as myself, I always came to myself as somebody else.

XLV

KATE

For as long as I can remember, I have thought that the sky was not all there was to see, but that if I took a sword and sliced open the heavens, the world would fall apart like two halves of an egg and I would be able to see into the heavens.

After having split into two people, I came back to myself, perched like a vulture on the railing of the bridge. Now I am waiting uselessly, endlessly for a visitor who will never arrive. I could slip a message in a bottle, but what could I say? I could not even frame it in the negative: 'I am not a prisoner.' I could not frame it in the negative because there is nothing left to negate. What else can I do? The way out has upped and left. Wherever I turn my head, there are eyes staring. Before I was never watched. Now I am watched.

XLVI

Jim

The lines which had run straight hooked themselves into patterns of hazed disorder. The map grew gnarled fingers and barbs where the roads had been. The rivers flooded their banks. The space between the towns weighed more than the towns. The white relief ornament which decorated the centre of the roof became a plaster eye decorated with fruit and flowers.

The black leather sofa sat washed up on the sand. The mermaid perched upon a rock, playing with a circle of shells and seaweed which hung around her neck. The man was jogging slowly along the beach. The new train lay with its wheels clogged with grey sand.

I mechanically rose to fix myself a cup of Earl Grey. Turn handle, two, three, four, down stairs, one through seven, click kettle on, wait for steam. I observe myself in the third person.

'Now he is taking out a teabag from the red cardboard box with yellow writing on the side. Now he is pouring water into the pot. Now he is placing the teabag into the boiling water. Now he is waiting for the tea to steep. Now he is taking a cup down from the cupboard behind him. Now he is pouring the tea into the cup.' The tea is hitting the side of the cup and trickling down into a milky brown ocean. Everything is slowing down in expectation of the big day.

One step, two step, she was behind me.

'A long sleep, a long sleep, that's all.'

He was all laid out in the wooden box. The gold handles seemed made of spun hair. Snow white in the glass coffin. Only this was real. I placed a rose beside my father and moved out into the corridor. Willy was howling from his room, so I ran in to see what was happening to him. Mother was standing over him as he jerked about on the floor like a wind-up clown.

'Call the doctor, call the doctor, call the doctor.'

I ran downstairs towards the telephone.

'Now he is walking up the stairs with the cup of tea in his hand. Now he is entering his bedroom, taking the black gown out of the wardrobe and laying it on the bed. He is looking at his watch. He is standing before the cracked looking glass and combing his hair. Now he is putting a record on to the turntable.'

'Call Doctor White. His number's at the back of the book.'

'Hello could you please come around to the Pearsons' house. It's my brother. He's locked up in some kind of fit. No, it hasn't happened before. I don't know. We can't calm him down. Yes, it may have been triggered by something. I can hear him howling. Please come quickly. My mother is very scared.'

I hung up the telephone and went outside on to the front porch. It was a grey kind of day, with little tufts of clouds being blown across the sky. The mud path leading to the gate had small pits in it from where last night's hail had fallen. I walked along to the path, Willy's voice floating out of the window and down to where I stood now at the gate. I hung over the iron gate and waited for the doctor to hurry up and come and make Willy get better.

'Is your brother better?'

'Yes Miss Clark.'

'I hear he had a bit of a nasty turn, after . . . and we're all very sorry about that.'

'Thank you, Miss Clark.'

'If your mother thinks it best that you have a couple of days off school, then that's all right by me. This is a time for you and your brother . . . well, for you to help your mother as much as possible. I want you to show Miss Clark that you are a brave little soldier.'

'Yes Miss Clark.'

'Good boy.'

She handed me a bunch of flowers which smelt of the rosewater my mother used.

The mermaid sat with a stick upon the rock island. She hooked up a saltwater trout. My father came over to where I was sitting and shook the sand out of the train.

'What are you doing with that out here? It'll get wrecked. Take it on back to the cabin. You can play with it there.'

I left the mermaid behind and walked up the beach to number nine. A small row of geraniums grew outside in a set of brown containers. I picked a pink flower and took it inside with me.

'He's sent me flowers!'

'I hate him.'

'Come on, Jim. You haven't even given him half a chance.'

'Don't have to give him even quarter of a chance to know that I'll hate him.'

'You can't expect me to stay dressed up in black like an old witch for ever!'

'Why not? We got along fine before *he* came along.'

'I think you're being very selfish.'

'Am not being selfish. *Dad* wouldn't have liked him.'

'You little shit. You're behaving like a seven-year-old.'

'So?'

'So I'm only asking for you to give him a fair go.'

'Why do you have to go out with a taxi driver? Why can't you go out with a multi-millionaire?'

'Because it's my life, and I'll go out with who I want.'

'It's not fair. He's gross.'

'He is not gross. He's a perfectly respectable man with a steady job who is willing to have a relationship with a woman with two sons, one of whom is severely disabled. If you can't learn to accept that, then it's tough bickies.'

'He never brings *me* presents.'

'Why should he?'

'He gave *you* flowers.'

'That's because he's my boyfriend.'

'Don't say that word! You're too old to have a boyfriend.'

'Rubbish. You're never too old.'

'Yuk.'

'Go and run round in the back yard. Go on, shoosh off and go and play at the neighbours.'

'Now he is moving into the bathroom and opening the medicine cabinet. Now he is removing a razor from the cabinet. He is foaming up his chin with soap in front of the bathroom mirror. Now he is shaving himself. He is undressing and stepping into the shower. He is washing himself and humming Wagner. Now he is drying off with a fish-patterned, brightly coloured towel.'

The mermaid had thrown the trout into the middle of the cabin. It couldn't breathe. It lay with its mouth opening and closing opening and closing opening. I stood on the belly of the fish. Closing. A ring of shells made a small circle around the fish. My father came into the room.

'Happy, little boy? Let's get this coil lit then. Don't want to be bitten to death.'

He stepped over the fish, put a green coil on the table. Smoke rose up in a thin stream, then spread about the ceiling.

The doctor came into the room where Willy was howling and held him down.

I drank one, I drank four, I drank ten. Then I was clutching an orange bottle, which wasn't alcohol, no it wasn't alcohol at all. It was really water just pretending to be alcohol. Time to go home. Shit be quiet shit tiptoe tippy tippy tiddly toe up the stairs, don't wake Red. 'Where the hell have you been?' Just playing bridge at a friend's house. Feeling a bit like puking . . . shit look out whoops must have been something I ate. Blackout whitelight morning. Oh God what did I do? My room stinks.

'Hope you're proud of yourself. Learnt your lesson well, I suppose. Your mother and I have decided to be quite decent about the whole thing and not punish you. Today'll be punishment enough, I should expect. You'll have to clean your own stains out of the carpet. Come on. Up and out of bed. Your Mum's made a good bit of egg and bacon for breakfast. Just what you'll feel like, eh?'

God, that smell. Think I'm gonna chuck.

'Somebody's learnt a good old lesson, eh? Can't put anything past your old Mum.'

'Corn's up! Pass the salt, would you Red? Jim! Stop swinging on that chair. You'll fall.'

'You were fine for the first five hundred kilometres. Why are you whinging now? You should have gone to the toilet when we last stopped. Don't be stupid, of course you can't get out now. You'll have to wait.'

'We were all very sorry. When we heard about it. Why don't you go on and read with the other boys. In the corner.'

There is a velveteen rope in the corner of the room. It lifts its head like a snake and rearranges its brown coils.

Everybody was standing on the trout, crushing the little shells. My father ate his corn like a typewriter one way ching-

ching along ching-ching. Underneath the table I had my marbles in a small flax bag. The top of it was tied with string.

'Did you pick up the tickets on your way home from varsity? Oh, great. Diana's bringing him home soon, so we'll bring out the cake and eat that, then someone can take him. He'll love it. Can you get the candles out of the pantry please, Jim?'

'Just fifteen?'

'That'll do it. Cheers. Red's finishing the shift early, so we can all celebrate together. This'll be one night you're not heading off to the pub with your mates. This'll be him . . . Oh, Willy, did you have a good birthday?'

'Hey, Will! What you been up to? Been for a walk to the shops?'

'See ya, Diana. Yep, same time tomorrow.'

'He thinks, "Tomorrow I'll be a free man." He packs the gown into a blue satchel and heads down the stairs and out of the door.

'Blow out the candles, Willy!'

'Fifteen! Don't time fly!'

'Go on, we're all as hungry as hell.'

My mother sliced off a large chunk of cake and handed it over to Willy who wolfed it down. He started to choke on the cake, which triggered off one of his fits.

'Medicine!'

I ran upstairs and got the brown bottle from Willy's room. As soon as the medicine went down his throat he became very calm and eventually lay completely still upon the kitchen floor.

'The town clock is chiming as he heads towards the hall.'

What's the time, Mr Wolf?

One o'clock.

What's the time, Mr Wolf?

Two o'clock.

What's the time, Mr Wolf?
Three o'clock.
What's the time, Mr Wolf?
Dinner time!

'Now a train is rattling past underneath him, and he spits on to the locomotive. He moves across to the other side and heads up the track that leads to the swimming hole. Time to waste, spare time, time on his hands. An hour equals sixty minutes equals three hundred and sixty seconds. Red and Mother will be waiting in the hall. Now he can see the swimming hole. Two girls are swimming. The first girl has blonde hair and the second has brown. He wishes he had his swimming togs on him so that he could go for a swim to help pass the time. He sits down on a small grassy ledge, takes a book out of his bag and begins to read.'

After about ten minutes he seemed to be all right, and we'd spent so much money on the tickets that we had to go to the circus. When he was unconscious Mum put the tickets into a little plastic container, and put the container inside the cake so that he might find them when he came right. He was hopping around excitedly: I'm sure he'd figured out where we were going. I said I'd take him, 'cause I kind of wanted to see the whole thing myself, even though I didn't want to tell my mates about it in case they hassled me about being eighteen and still being into kids' stuff. So we dressed up real warm and ran all the way to the park, with some neighbour's old mutt chasing along after us like a blind shadow yapping at our heels. The lake was completely frozen over, which kind of spooked Willy out, but as soon as we got into the big top and I'd bought him a toffee apple he was fine.

The velveteen rope swelled and expanded until it became an antelope. Mother came in with the doctor. I told them about the antelope.

I wasn't going to tell anybody about my bag of

marbles that the lady had given me. I wanted to bury them in the magic forest behind the cabin. It was the same magic forest that was in the book. I would bury my little bag with the trout, and the mermaid would guard over them. Not even Willy would know, but I would bury one for him.

I told them about the map with the hooks and barbs.

The raven was caught in the fence. I poked at it with a stick and black dust flew up in a puff of air. I climbed over the fence and walked into the blanket of red pine needles.

'He reads for about half an hour, then decides it is time to leave. He passes over the trains, then heads for the hall. He enters by a small door at the back, where the other students sit waiting, already in costume. He gets flustered, and changes into his costume very quickly. He says his name to the dean, who writes it at the bottom of a long list. He slips into his black gown and holds his cap between his hands. The tassels hang down.'

The antelope changes back into a rope which the doctor uses to monitor my heart rate. My heart sits in my chest, pumping blood to my hands who clench and unclench themselves at Willy.

'How long?'

'Are your folks in the audience?'

'What are we up to?'

'Abrahms.'

'Jesus Christ. Wake me up when we get to Paull.'

'Just talk to him as an ordinary human being, that's all he wants.'

'He's not a human being. He's hairy and ugly and he drives taxis.'

'I'm sick of this conversation. It's ended. You'll have to like him or lump him, because he's staying around, no matter what you say.'

'Don't I have any say?'

'No.'

'But Mum! He's revolting! Why did you have to pick *him*?'

'I *said*, this discussion is now ended. If you had a girlfriend I wouldn't tell you she was revolting.'

'Girls are revolting anyway.'

'That's not what you'll be saying in a few years from now.'

'Paterson, Paton, Paull, Pearce, Pearson.'

'Shit, that's me.'

'Now he is sitting at the bottom of the stairs, waiting for the others to walk up on to the stage ahead of him. Now he is ascending the stairs. Now he is walking across the stage. Now he is accepting his degree. "James Pearson, BA English Literature."

'Now he is putting on his cap. Now he is walking off the stage and down the opposite staircase. Now he is moving backstage.'

'Please, can I go now. I'm busting!'

'You saw the sign! There's a rest area five hundred metres up the road.'

'I don't want to go in five hundred metres, I want to go now!'

'Listen to your mother!'

'Willy wants to go too, don't you Willy?'

'Look, you only have to hold on for a hundred more metres now.'

'He'll hold on through all of this, Mrs Pearson, don't you worry. He'll emerge out the other side a fine and healthy young man. Has he been under a lot of stress or pressure lately?'

'Yes. A death in the family.'

'Well now, that'll take some getting over. That's not the kind of thing that just goes away overnight. For now, I think the best thing is rest. But later on, you must attempt to take him out of himself. Is he introverted by nature?'

'No . . . not really.'

'Look.'

Rustle, rustle, rustle.

'There's obviously some sort of cognitive malfunction at the moment. Why don't you give him two of these daily, and he might snap to his senses. Oh . . . I mean they might help him to recover from this shock. Chemical imbalance, you know, Mrs Pearson, can be responsible for a lot of bizarre behaviour. Hallucinations, delusions of grandeur, major depressive disorder, manic depression . . . oh, mind, I'm not saying that your son has any of these, but rather that these drugs restore order to chemical chaos. Ah-hem.'

Clear throat again. Shuffle two steps to left. Give small, stagey cough. Shuffle one pace to right.

'For now I recommend the medication, for later . . . I recommend plenty of physical activity, and nothing too straining on the cerebral capacities. Don't you think?'

'I don't quite know what to say, to tell you the truth.'

'Any history of mental illness in the family?'

'None.'

'And the boy's father?'

'Died when Jim was ten.'

'That can't have been easy on a young lad.'

'It was trying for all of us.'

'How old is he now, Mrs Pearson, if you don't mind me asking, that is.'

'He's twenty-one.'

'Is he employed?'

'No. He has a degree in English Literature. He graduated earlier this year.'

'Jobs can't be too easy for a fellow with an English degree. The stock exchange seems rather disinterested in the downfall of Madame Bovary at the moment.'

'So it would seem.'

'But he's looking for work?'

'Yes, he hunts . . . or he hunted, every day.'

'Good. Good. I'm sure he'll be right soon enough and making somebody a fine little assistant in some field or another, no doubt.'

'Thank you. I'll see you out.'

'Lovely.'

I thought about him. I thought about how he had gone somewhere else. I thought about him being with my father now. Then I didn't think any more.

'Here we are. You can get out now.'

I ran into the bushes and peed against a rock. Red was revving the engine impatiently.

'Hurry up, Jim. We haven't got all bloody day.'

'Coming!'

I ran back to the car, leapt in and slammed the door. Willy was curled up in a small ball, sucking a strand of his hair.

'How much longer now?'

'Two skips, a hop and a jump.'

'Are we getting the same cabin?'

Nobody said anything.

'Too many memories, Jim.'

'I liked that cabin. Do you remember that coil that Dad burnt to keep away the mosquitoes?'

'No. We're getting a different cabin, and that's the last I want to hear about it.'

'I want to see if anything's changed.'

'That was five years ago. You were only seven. Of course things have changed.'

'Can I go and look at our old cabin?'

'If you want. Right. I spy with my little eye, something beginning with . . .'

It was near twelve. The plaster eye was still shining down. Nothing was happening here. Nothing moved. In the snow outside, a bronze effigy was being burnt in the street. Boys in red woolly hats and snow shoes gathered around to throw straw and sticks on to the flaming pile, leaving footprints in the snow. The first stroke of midnight sounded. The mirror walked to the other side of the room. Taps of a hammer rose up from the street. Nobody was in the room. The maidenhair fern which sat on my table threw itself on to the floor and lay in a smashed heap of dirt and crockery. The chair reshuffled its legs.

I struggled from beneath the blankets of cotton wool and worked my way down the stairs, clutching the wooden banister.

Patricia stood gazing out of the window which was positioned above the kitchen sink. The clock tower chimed again.

'Will you never get to the circus?'

She looked at me silently. Petal and the bride came up behind her. The bride handed Patricia a red rose. She took it and clasped it between her hands. Somebody was hammering on the front door. When I pulled it open I saw Ringer standing in the pouring rain, rivulets of water streaming down his face.

'The court case was this morning. My charge has been reduced to manslaughter. Kylo's in the cell next to mine. Got done for aiding and abetting, didn't he.'

A police car on the street tooted twice.

'So, I still haven't served my time then. Come and visit, eh?'

He ran into the driving rain, sending steams of water out behind him. Everything was winding up most conveniently.

When I returned to the kitchen I saw the bride and Patricia standing in the sink, the dirty dishwater half-way up to their knees. Patricia bent down and pulled out the plug. I watched as they spiralled down the drain, leaving behind only frothy suds of Sunlight and some dark coffee grinds. Their shadows flickered briefly on the wall, and then were gone. I took a glass jar down from the top shelf, and scooped the coffee grinds into it. Tomorrow I would bury it at the graveyard.

I climbed the staircase, left hand on the banister. I had best be getting back to my manuscripts or I might never escape alone to Paris.

The twelfth stroke of midnight sounds.

Somebody is at the door. I feel a hand on my shoulder, and turn around to face my shadow.

'Hello,' she says.

We step up on to the bed, and into the dark.

The chair was empty. The letter was dead.

The lamp was silent. The lamp was black.